The Return of the Dragon

The Return of the Dragon

Rebecca Rupp

CANDLEWICK PRESS
CAMBRIDGE, MASSACHUSETTS

Copyright © 2005 by Rebecca Rupp

First paperback edition 2006

The Library of Congress has cataloged the hardcover edition as follows:

Rupp, Rebecca.
The return of the dragon / by Rebecca Rupp. — 1st ed.
p. cm.
Summary: Hannah, Zachary, and Sarah Emily return to Lonely Island
to save their friend Fafnyr, a three-headed dragon, from being captured
by a rich man who wants to put the creature on display.
ISBN 0-7636-2377-6 (hardcover)
[1. Dragons—Fiction. 2. Brothers and sisters—Fiction. 3. Islands—Fiction.] I. Title.
PZ7.R8886Re 2005
[Fic]—dc22   2004045184

ISBN 0-7636-2804-2 (paperback)

2 4 6 8 10 9 7 5 3 1

Printed in the United States of America

This book was typeset in Berkeley Oldstyle.

Candlewick Press
2067 Massachusetts Avenue
Cambridge, Massachusetts 02140

visit us at www.candlewick.com

For dragon lovers everywhere

1

Back to Lonely Island

"Zachary! Sarah Emily!"

Twelve-year-old Hannah dashed up the stairs, shouting for her younger brother and sister. Zachary—who was almost eleven—and Sarah Emily, who was nine, were sitting on the floor in Zachary's room, playing Monopoly. Zachary had just made a shrewd bargain involving Atlantic Avenue and the Electric Company, when they heard Hannah's voice.

"We're in here!" Sarah Emily called.

The door flew open and Hannah burst in. Her brown eyes were bright and her cheeks pink with excitement.

"Something wonderful has happened!" she exclaimed. "Mother just told me. She and Dad are going to Europe during our spring vacation."

"Europe!" said Sarah Emily. She peered at Hannah owlishly through her thick spectacles.

"Are we going too?" asked Zachary.

"It's even better," said Hannah. "We're going to Aunt Mehitabel's house on Lonely Island. And this time Aunt Mehitabel is coming with us."

Zachary let out a whoop of glee. Hannah sank down on the bed, shoving aside a pile of computer manuals and the scattered pieces of Zachary's latest model rocket. She was grinning from ear to ear.

"There's an International Whale Conference in London," she said. "Father is going to give a speech there. Mother is going with him, and after the meeting, they're going to take a vacation by themselves. A second honeymoon. But they're worried that we're going to feel bad if they go without us."

"I'd rather go to the island," Sarah Emily said.

"So would I," said Hannah. Her eyes turned toward the map of Lonely Island that hung on the wall above Zachary's bed. "I can't wait to get back to Drake's Hill and see—"

"*Shh!*" Zachary said. He reached across the Monopoly board, upsetting Sarah Emily's two fortress-like hotels on Park Place, and grabbed Hannah's ankle. "We promised to keep him *secret* and *safe*, remember? We shouldn't even say his name out loud."

"I don't see why not," Hannah said.

"There's nobody around," Sarah Emily said.

"That doesn't matter," Zachary said darkly. "We have to get into the habit. Spies could be anywhere."

"Well, not *here*," Hannah said.

"That's the thing about spies," Zachary said ominously. "They show up where you least expect them."

Zachary had been reading a book about secret agents who carried tiny cameras the size of gumdrops and had microphones that could pick up whispered conversations half a mile away.

"We should come up with some kind of code name for him, so we can talk without anybody knowing what's going on. We could just call him F, like Aunt Mehitabel does in her letters."

"It's been so long," Sarah Emily said. "Sometimes I'm almost afraid that we dreamed the whole thing."

Hannah stretched out her hand. In the center of her palm glittered a tiny pinprick of gold.

"Just look at your hand," she said.

Zachary and Sarah Emily glanced down at their hands, where identical golden flecks gleamed.

Then Zachary quickly closed his fist, hiding the mysterious golden spark from sight.

"*Secret,*" he said.

The next weeks dragged by. It seemed as if vacation would never come. Then, just a week before leaving, an unexpected letter arrived from Aunt Mehitabel, written in swooping handwriting in lavender ink.

"Oh, no," said Mother as she read it. "This is dreadful news."

"What's happened?" asked Hannah anxiously.

"Aunt Mehitabel won't be able to go to the island with you after all," Mother said. "She's had a fall and has broken her ankle. She's all right, she says, but she will be laid up for several weeks while it heals. She's terribly disappointed. There's a letter enclosed for you children."

She handed the children an envelope and hurried away to the telephone. The letter was addressed to Hannah, Zachary, and Sarah Emily. It was sealed with emerald-green sealing wax and was marked PRIVATE.

"Open it," Sarah Emily said, tugging on Hannah's arm.

Hannah broke the seal, tore the envelope open, and pulled out a single folded sheet of paper:

Dear Children,

I am _furious_ to have had this foolish accident, which will prevent me from spending time with you this vacation! I was _so looking forward_ to it! In the meantime, Mr. and Mrs. Jones will look after you, and you, I trust, will look after our _mutual friend_. Please give F my regrets and fondest wishes.

Yours affectionately,

Aunt Mehitabel

"Oh, how awful," said Hannah.

"Poor Aunt Mehitabel," said Sarah Emily.

Mother bustled back into the room, shaking her head. She gave the children a rueful smile. "She fell out of a tree, bird watching," she said. "Why Aunt Mehitabel thought she could climb a tree at her age, with her arthritis . . . But she's going to be fine. And you children will have a lovely time with Mr. and Mrs. Jones."

Mr. and Mrs. Jones were the only people who lived on Lonely Island. They looked after Aunt Mehitabel's house. Mr. Jones went back and forth to the mainland to fetch mail and groceries in his boat, the *Martha,* and Mrs. Jones was a wonderful cook.

"I hope she's made doughnuts," said Zachary longingly.

"Oatmeal cookies," said Sarah Emily promptly.

"I hope you'll find something to do on the island besides eat," Mother said worriedly. "It's still chilly there this time of year. It's much too cold to swim."

"Don't worry," said Hannah. "We'll find plenty to do."

Mother and Father took the children to Chadwick, Maine, to meet Mr. Jones before leaving themselves for the airport in Boston. Mr. Jones was waiting on the wharf when they arrived. He had red cheeks and a bushy gray beard that made him look a little bit like Santa Claus. The children flung themselves on him.

"How is Mrs. Jones?"

"Do you still have Buster?"

Buster was the Joneses' cat, a fat gray tabby.

"Can I run the *Martha*?" That was Zachary.

There were last-minute instructions from Mother and Father and hugs all around. Then the children and Mr. Jones climbed into the boat, and Zachary cast off. They watched, waving, as their parents grew smaller in the distance. Sarah Emily sniffled.

"I hate goodbyes," she said.

"Me, I never think of it as 'goodbye,'" Mr. Jones said. "I think of it as 'until we meet again.' And look, there she is ahead of you. There's Lonely Island."

The children leaned forward, eager for their first glimpse of Aunt Mehitabel's house.

"I see it!" Sarah Emily shouted. "There's the weathervane!"

The familiar house came slowly into view, an old gray Victorian with a wide veranda, tall tower, and widow's walk, topped with a whirling metal weathervane shaped like a ship under full sail. Mrs. Jones was waiting for them at the open front door. She hugged each of the children in turn and told them all how much they'd grown, even Sarah Emily, who was convinced that she hadn't grown at all.

"You know which bedrooms are yours," Mrs. Jones declared. "Scoot up and get settled."

The children paused on the way upstairs to peek into Aunt Mehitabel's front parlor. It was just as they remembered. The windows were hung with green velvet curtains, and one wall was covered by a Chinese lacquer cabinet, with gold trees painted on its doors. There were straight-backed chairs with needlepoint seat covers, tiny end tables with spindly legs, a stool made out of an elephant's foot, and a horsehair sofa that always reminded the children of a stuffed walrus.

"There's the telescope, Zachary," said Sarah Emily. Zachary loved the telescope, which had belonged to the sea captain who originally built Aunt Mehitabel's house.

"There's your favorite, Hannah," teased Zachary, pointing at the elephant's-foot stool.

Hannah made a horrible face.

"I hate that thing," she said. "It has *toes*. But I love everything else. It feels just like home."

"It does, doesn't it?" said Sarah Emily. "It's as if we'd never been away."

Later, after the clothes were unpacked and put in drawers, and the empty suitcases were shoved under beds, they gathered in the kitchen. As they munched

Mrs. Jones's oatmeal cookies and drank steaming mugs of cocoa, they heard all the latest news of the island.

"We heard about your auntie's busted ankle," Mr. Jones said. "She was right sorry not to be here with you while your folks are off in London."

"Mother says she's doing fine," said Hannah. "She just won't be able to walk around for quite a while."

"A real shame," said Mrs. Jones.

"I'm sorry she's not here, too," said Mr. Jones. "We've had a bit of excitement here. Visitors. We haven't met them yet, but their boat is anchored up off the north end of the island. Near that pile of rocks you youngsters are all so fond of. Drake's Hill."

$\mathcal{O}$ 2 $\mathcal{O}$

Intruders on the Beach

"It's probably perfectly all right," Hannah said later, as the children met in Zachary's room before going to bed. "Just fishermen or something. Nobody could possibly know about—"

"Careful," Zachary said warningly.

"About F," Hannah finished.

"His cave isn't easy to find," said Sarah Emily. "Nobody could find it, could they? Unless they knew right where to look?"

She was clutching Oberon, the stuffed yellow elephant who had slept with her since she was two years old. Oberon had one ear and button eyes that bulged nervously when Sarah Emily squeezed him too hard. Just now Oberon looked very nervous.

"I don't like it," Zachary said. "It could be dangerous, strangers poking around. They could be *spies*. They could have some kind of laser-powered eye that can see right through rock."

"Oh, stop it, Zachary," Hannah said. "I wish you'd never read that stupid book. You're scaring S.E." She patted Oberon on the head, then put her arm around Sarah Emily and gave her a little squeeze. "Don't worry," she said. "Everything is probably fine."

"Sure," Zachary said. But he didn't sound convinced.

"You'll see," Hannah said. "We'll go first thing in the morning and investigate."

"I wish we could go tonight," Sarah Emily said.

Sarah Emily opened her eyes to sun pouring across her pillow. Zachary was shaking her foot.

She sat up, rubbing her eyes. Zachary was already dressed, though he hadn't brushed his sandy-colored hair, which was standing on end all over his head. It made him look like a hedgehog with freckles.

"Hurry up and get dressed," he said. "It's too great a day to waste. We can get going right after breakfast."

They found Mrs. Jones scrambling eggs in the kitchen, her pink apron covering a pair of faded overalls. A plate of blueberry muffins steamed on the table. Buster was asleep in the kitchen rocking chair, lying on his back with his paws in the air.

Sarah Emily was too excited to eat, and she glared at Zachary as he reached for his fourth muffin.

"I thought you were in a hurry," she said impatiently.

"I am," Zachary said. "But I'm growing. I need fuel."

He ate his muffin in two enormous gulps. Hannah shook her head at him.

As soon as the table was cleared, they shouted good-bye and thanks to Mrs. Jones, and flew out the back door, racing for the garden gate. Zachary, who liked to be well supplied, wore a bulging backpack containing a bag of snacks, a flashlight, a pair of binoculars, his Swiss army knife, a notebook, and a mechanical pencil. Alert to the possibility of spies, he had also added a magnifying glass and the hand-held tape recorder that he had been given for his last birthday.

"You look like a camel," Sarah Emily said.

"A camel stuffed with muffins," said Hannah.

It was a beautiful day. They found the familiar path, a narrow worn track leading toward the rising hill at the far end of the island. The hill looked silent and empty, dark against the bright blue sky. The children hastened toward it.

They stopped for a snack at the halfway point, then hurried on, following the little path through thickets, around boulders, and across open fields. Finally Drake's Hill loomed above them. It was dotted with clumps of dark green fir trees, some twisted into strange shapes by the sea wind, and at the very top was a vast blocky pile of gray rock, looking like a tumbled tower built by a careless giant. They paused, gazing upward, breathing hard.

Suddenly Zachary put his hand on Hannah's arm. "Wait a minute," he said. "Someone's been here."

"Oh, Zachary, not *spies* again," Hannah said.

"Well, look," Zachary said.

The girls followed his pointing finger. The flat field at the foot of the hill was brown with withered weeds and grass—it was still too early for the green of spring— and through it a faint track led to the right, winding around the base of the hill toward the beach.

"Rabbits?" asked Sarah Emily hopefully.

Zachary shook his head. "Too big," he said. "Somebody's been making a path. See that? That's a heel mark."

"Let's follow it," Hannah said.

The track skirted the base of the hill and ended in a little cluster of trees. Beyond the trees, the children could hear the steady crash of ocean waves on the distant beach.

"I told you it was rabbits," Sarah Emily said.

Suddenly Hannah, in the lead, stopped dead.

"Look at that!" she said in a horrified voice.

Zachary and Sarah Emily crowded behind her, staring.

Someone had made a campsite on the beach. A cluster of white tents was set up behind the sheltering rise of a dune. There were five tents, one much larger than the others. "That must be the leader's," Zachary whispered.

The large tent had plastic windows in it—they could be sealed shut at night with white canvas covers—and a zippered double door. A folding wooden chair was set just outside the door with a table next to it. On the other side of the chair was a tripod to which was attached an enormous pair of black binoculars.

As the children watched, crouching behind the tree trunks, the zippered door rolled open and an elderly Chinese man came out. He was tall and thin, dressed in a black suit, with an embroidered cap on his head. He stood silently, his expression grim, eyes narrowed to slits, arms folded across his chest. Then he stalked slowly across the campsite and vanished between the tents, heading in the direction of the sea.

"Who's *that*?" Sarah Emily said. She sounded frightened.

Hannah and Zachary exchanged anxious glances.

"A trespasser," Zachary said.

They watched the camp for several more minutes, but nothing happened. The tents sat silent and deserted, their canvas doors firmly shut.

"We might as well go," Hannah whispered finally.

The children turned and crept quietly back through the trees, the way that they had come.

"Let's go see . . . F," Zachary said. "We should warn him about this."

❦ 3 ❦

The Hidden Cave

The children hurriedly retraced their steps, putting as much space as possible between themselves and the white tents on the beach.

"So who lives in those tents?" Zachary fretted. "And *where* are they? They could be anywhere. *Spying.*"

"Oh, do be quiet, Zachary," Hannah said. "Let's climb."

They scrambled up the steep slope of Drake's Hill until they reached the enormous pile of rock, layered like gigantic steps, that crowned the hilltop. Carefully they began to climb, feeling for remembered hand- and foot-holds. At last they edged around a final rocky ledge to stand on a wide platform overlooking the ocean. At the back of the platform gaped a dark opening that led, the children knew, to a hidden cave. The very sight of it made their hearts beat faster. Before them was an endless stretch of deep blue water, lashed by the wind into white-capped waves. And just off the shore of the island—

"Look at *that*!" gasped Zachary, pointing downward.

Below them, a great white boat lay at anchor.

"A yacht," said Hannah in an awed voice.

"I'll bet that's who's camping on the beach," Zachary said.

He fumbled in his backpack and pulled out his own small pair of binoculars. He put them to his eyes, focused, and slowly swept the length of the boat, from bow to stern.

"Funny," he said. "It doesn't have a name. Most boats have names. Even Mr. Jones's little boat has a name painted on it. But this one doesn't say anything. It's just plain white."

"Let me see," said Hannah, reaching for the binoculars.

She put them to her eyes and studied the silent floating yacht.

Then, as the children watched, a doorway opened and a man appeared on the yacht's polished deck. He was broad-shouldered and deeply tanned, with closely clipped iron-gray hair. He wore dark trousers and a heavy white sweater. He stood for a moment gazing out to sea, then slowly turned toward the island. A seagull glided past, sun glinting off its white wings. The man lifted a pair of binoculars to his eyes. Hastily the children dropped down behind a pile of concealing boulders.

15

"*He's watching F's cave,*" Zachary said. "He suspects something."

"How could he?" Hannah said in disgusted tones. "You're nuts, Zachary. He was watching that gull."

"It gives me the creeps," said Zachary. "That boat. Those tents. People snooping around."

Cautiously he poked his head above the rocks and peered toward the white yacht. The gray-haired man had lowered his binoculars and was scribbling something in a small notebook.

"You see?" Hannah said. "He's a bird watcher. They take notes all the time. About the kinds of birds they've sighted."

"I think he's going below," Zachary said. "There—he's walking across the deck—he's gone."

"Let's go see Fafnyr," Hannah said. And then, as Zachary frowned and opened his mouth: "I *know*, Zachary, but all this *F* stuff is getting silly. We'll ask him if he knows anything about the boat. And the camp."

Zachary dropped the binoculars back in his pack and pulled out his flashlight.

"Let's go," he said. "I'll lead the way."

One by one, the three children ducked into the cave. As they entered, they smelled the special scent remembered from last summer—a spicy mix of wood smoke, incense, and cinnamon. The cave was much larger than it looked from the outside. Zachary's flashlight threw eerie shadows on the stone walls. As they edged farther into the cave, the sounds of the outside world were suddenly silenced. The whistle of the wind and the rhythmic crash of the waves ceased abruptly. All was utterly quiet. The cave led farther and farther downward, deep into the center of the hill.

"The cave seems bigger than it used to," Sarah Emily said. Her voice quavered a little. Sarah Emily was afraid of the dark.

"It's all right," Zachary said reassuringly in front of her. "We're almost there."

Just as he finished speaking, there was a brilliant glitter in the darkness as the flashlight beam reflected off a broad expanse of shining golden scales.

Sarah Emily caught her breath.

It was a dragon.

4

Fafnyr

The dragon's name, the children knew, was Fafnyr Goldenwings. Fafnyr was a tridrake—a three-headed dragon—who had been alive for thousands of years. The cave was a Resting Place, a safe haven for dragons, given to Fafnyr long ago by Aunt Mehitabel when she was a little girl. Aunt Mehitabel, who was in her eighties, seldom visited the island now. She lived in an apartment in Philadelphia. Just last summer, she had given the children clues that helped them discover the dragon. "The time has come," Aunt Mehitabel had written them in a letter, "for me to pass on the trust. I am not getting any younger and Fafnyr needs friends and protectors." The children had promised to keep Fafnyr and his Resting Place secret and safe. In return, they had all become Dragon Friends, marked by the dragon's claw in the center of their palms with a spark of shining gold.

There was the sound of a heavy body shifting on the cave floor. Then there came a soft hiss in the darkness as the dragon, awakened, softly flamed. The cave blossomed into light. A pair of neon-green eyes opened, at first narrowed into gleaming slits, then growing wider.

"Fafnyr," breathed Zachary.

The dragon made a rumbling sound deep in its chest and brushed a golden claw across its eyes. It arched its neck, unfolded its smooth golden wings, and stretched them out one at a time, first to the right and then to the left.

"Dear me. I must have dozed off," it said in a scratchy voice. It cleared its throat.

"How nice to see you all again," it said. It nodded majestically to each child. "Hannah. Zachary. Sarah Emily. Delightful."

"It's wonderful to see you, Fafnyr," Hannah said. "We've missed you terribly. It has been months and months since we've been here."

The dragon gave a jaw-cracking yawn.

"I have missed you too, my dears," it said. It cleared its throat again in an embarrassed manner. "Or," it added, "I would have, if I had been awake. I do need my rest, you understand."

The dragon yawned enormously for a second time.

"Months, you say," it said. "How time flies. And what have you been doing since we saw you last?"

"Oh, we've been at school," said Hannah. "We haven't been doing anything important. I'm taking art classes. And I'm on the field hockey team."

"And you, dear boy?" The golden head turned toward Zachary.

"I've been building model rockets," Zachary said. "I named the best one after you, Fafnyr. I painted it a sort of gold color, so I named it Goldenwings. You should see it fly."

"Is it the kind that explodes?" the dragon asked in a delighted voice. "I always liked the ones that explode. A bang, and then all those glittery bits."

"Those are fireworks," said Zachary. "These are different. They have engines. You launch them and then they come back down on parachutes."

"Ah," the dragon said. It rolled its eyes briefly upward in the direction of the cave ceiling, as if looking for a descending parachute.

Then it turned toward Sarah Emily. "And you, my dear?" it asked. "How have you been?"

"I've been fine," said Sarah Emily. "I'm taking piano lessons." She wrinkled her nose. "But I'm not very good yet. I'm only up to a thing called 'The Happy Froggie.'"

"Practice makes perfect," the dragon said. "I have no doubt that you will shortly triumph over this . . . cheerful amphibian." It hummed a few bars of something unrecognizable. "I myself have musical ambitions," it confided. "We must collaborate sometime. Perhaps a duet."

"Fafnyr," Zachary cut in worriedly, "did you know there are strangers on the island? They're camping on the beach, right near the bottom of the hill. And there's a big boat anchored offshore—with a man on it who's watching your cave. Have you seen him? Do you know what he's doing here?"

"He could be dangerous," Sarah Emily said.

"He could be a *spy*," Zachary said.

Hannah sighed.

"We don't know that he's watching the cave," she said fairly. "We couldn't tell what he was looking at. Lots of people have binoculars. He could be a bird watcher."

The dragon thought for a moment.

"Has this . . . boat person . . . done anything frightening?" it asked finally. "Threatened you?"

"Well, no," said Zachary. "We just saw him looking at the hill through binoculars."

"So he *could*, in fact, be bird watching," the dragon said. "Or perhaps he's a student of rock formations. Or a landscape painter."

"Well," Zachary said doubtfully, "I guess he could be. We didn't really see him do anything wrong."

"I don't think Aunt Mehitabel would like trespassers," Sarah Emily said stubbornly. "Besides, he scared me."

The dragon slowly shook its head and made a tutting sound.

"It seems to me," it said judiciously, "that this person—these persons—are nothing to worry about. We should give them the benefit of the doubt. Innocent until proven guilty, you know. Doubtless they will shortly realize that this is a private island and will then depart. The situation will resolve itself."

"But what if they don't?" Sarah Emily asked. "Depart, I mean."

"Humans," the dragon said loftily, "waste inordinate amounts of time worrying about things that never happen and dangers that aren't really there."

"But the man *is* there," Sarah Emily protested. "And all those tents and things—"

Hannah put a restraining hand on her arm. "I don't think that's what Fafnyr means," she said. "He means you're imagining that the man on the boat is dangerous when he might not be at all. It's a little like Mrs. Bernini, remember?"

"Mrs. Bernini?" the dragon repeated.

Sarah Emily nodded. "She lives in a funny little house at the end of our street back home," she told the dragon. "I used to be really scared of her. She always wore black dresses and her yard was all tangly and full of weeds. I thought she was a witch. But she wasn't at all. Once we got to know her, she was really nice."

"She makes peanut brittle," Zachary said.

"Precisely," said the dragon. "Precisely, my dear. You worried foolishly about something that was never there. And what *was* there?"

It waved a triumphant claw.

"Peanut brittle," it said.

Zachary shuffled his feet restlessly. "But it never hurts to be careful," he said. "We promised Aunt Mehitabel to keep the Resting Place secret and safe."

The dragon gave a little sigh. "This all reminds me . . ." it said. It wriggled its wings and settled itself more comfortably on the cave floor.

"Perhaps," it said diffidently, "you would like to hear a story? It may help put your fears at rest."

"We'd love to," said Hannah.

"We've missed your stories," said Sarah Emily.

The children sat down on the cave's stone floor, snugly warmed by the dragon's inner fire, and leaned back against Fafnyr's golden tail. As the dragon began to speak, the cave walls seemed to shimmer and fade. There was a scent of dust and sun-warmed leaves—a foreign smell with a tang of licorice and lemon—and the twittering sounds of bird song and the *baa*-ing of sheep. The children, transported by the dragon's voice, found themselves swept into another place and time, seeing the world through someone else's eyes.

5

The Green-Eyed Dragon's Story
NIKO

"Niko," the dragon began, "was a shepherd boy. He lived long ago in the rocky hills of Greece, in the days when poets sang songs about gods and wars, and the great city of Athens, with its marble temples and crowded marketplace, seemed to be the very center of the world. Niko did not live in the city, though. He lived in a cottage in a little village, with his mother and father and his younger sister, Daphne. Around their cottage grew olive and lemon trees. Niko's father fished in the sea and brought home a good catch every night, while Niko tended the family's little flock of sheep, which wandered every day on the mountainside. But then one day trouble came to the village. . . ."

Niko, perched on a rock overlooking his flock of nine sheep and four new lambs, was worried. It was a beautiful day, warm and lazy, the sort of day that Niko usually liked to spend napping in the sun or sitting in the shade of the trees, daydreaming of all the things he'd like to do or be. Perhaps someday he would be the captain of a swift red-sailed ship, traveling to strange and distant lands and coming home laden with gold and silver and jewels. Or a great warrior in a glittering helmet topped with dyed horsetails, setting off to battle the Persians. Or best of all, a brilliant philosopher in a long white robe, discovering the answers to all his many questions: What are the stars made of? What causes rainbows? Why does the moon change shape? And—if a boy built himself a huge pair of feathered wings—would he be able to fly?

Today, however, all the questions seemed to have flown out of his mind. He was wide awake and alert, his eyes fearfully scanning every rock and tree, the fingers of his right hand pleating and re-pleating the hem of his short tunic. A monster was loose on the mountain.

First, sheep had begun to disappear. Two had vanished from the flock of Niko's friend Stephanos—simply gone without a trace. Soon more sheep were spirited away—one here, two there—almost, the shepherds claimed, between one blink of an eye and the next. Clumps of bloody wool were found caught in the bushes, and there were strange plots of crushed plants and broken branches—marks where something heavy had crouched, waiting for a chance to kill.

Then one of the villagers, a man named Jason, actually *saw* the monster. The creature was like no animal ever seen on earth, Jason said, gesturing wildly with his hands. It was a supernatural being with the body of a serpent, the wings of an eagle, and the head of a lion, yellow-fanged, with flaming red eyes. When Jason bravely approached it, dagger drawn, ready to do battle, the creature magically disappeared. He had found its enormous tracks in the soft ground, he told his awed listeners, but the tracks simply ceased at the point where the monster had vanished. Unfortunately a heavy rain in the night washed away the telltale traces. When he led the villagers to the very spot on the following day, there was nothing to be seen.

Now Niko, his heart pounding at the stir of every leaf and every rustle in the bushes, was afraid. He felt cold, even in the hot sun. He longed to take his flock and go home—but "Sheep have to eat," his father said. So here he was, waiting on the mountainside, with a scary prickly feeling between his shoulder blades.

Slowly the sun topped the sky and began its long

journey downward toward the horizon. Usually as he followed the sun's path across the sky, Niko thought about the sun god, Helios, driving his fiery chariot toward his shining palace in the west. But today he just waited impatiently for the day to be over and the sun to be gone. As the sun sank lower and lower, he gave a sigh of relief. Nothing had happened. The monster had not appeared. It was time to call his flock and go home.

He hurried across the field, gathering the sheep together for the trip down the mountain, to the safe pen behind the little house. He counted the sheep as he urged them along toward home. One, two, three, four, five—that was Daphne's favorite, a fat ewe with a comical black splotch over her nose—six, seven, eight, and nine. All were there. And then the four lambs, frisking about at their mothers' heels. Niko had named each one. There was plump little Penelope; Dido, who had a crumpled ear; Ajax, who was always causing trouble; and his own special lamb, Panno, who had soft brown wool, just the color of fresh-baked bread. One, two, three . . . Niko paused, frowning, and counted again. Three. Just three. His heart gave a thump of alarm. Panno was missing.

He rapidly circled the grazing field, peering under bushes and behind rocks, and calling. Behind him, one sheep began to bleat, and then another. Still no lamb.

The monster could strike between one blink of an eye and the next, Niko remembered, with an awful sinking feeling in his stomach. Had it been here, after all? Had it somehow crept to the edge of the field and lain there, watching him through the thicket with its flame-pointed red eyes? Niko shivered. But he had to try to find Panno. Quickly he collected his flock and drove them down the hill, through the little village street, and into the family sheep pen. He made sure their water trough was filled, then fastened the gate behind him and ran to poke his head in the cottage door. He explained the dreadful news to his mother.

"Wait for your father," his mother protested, but Niko shook his head.

"Maybe he hasn't gone far," he said. "I'll go look again. It won't be dark for a while yet."

He ran back down the village street and up the winding track toward the mountain. Once again he circled the field where his sheep had been grazing. Nothing there. He climbed higher, poking his head into every little thicket, checking behind every rock and tree. Then, caught and tangled in a thorny branch, he found a tiny tuft of soft brown wool. Panno must have wandered this way, Niko thought. Lost and confused. He called, but there was no answering *baa*. He climbed higher and higher, searching as he climbed. He had never explored this part of the mountain before. The shepherds stayed lower down, closer to the village, where the grass was greener and richer.

Suddenly he heard a shifting in the bushes in front of him, a scrabble on the rocks. Little hooves on stone? "Panno?" he called softly. He pushed the branches aside and felt his heart leap in terror in his chest. He was face-to-face with the monster.

It was the most enormous creature Niko had ever seen—bigger and more terrible than he had imagined. It was covered with gleaming golden scales. It had polished golden claws, a long arrow-pointed tail, wings neatly folded across its glittering back, and—Niko gasped—three heads on long serpent-like necks. One head, its eyes a piercing green, was looking directly at Niko. The other two heads, eyes closed, were curled low on the creature's shoulders, seemingly fast asleep. Niko's knees gave way beneath him. He sank to the ground and buried his face in his hands. He was almost too terrified to breathe.

Then the monster spoke.

"My dear boy," it said. It sounded concerned and upset. "Please don't be frightened." It nervously twitched its golden tail. "Despite my impressive and powerful appearance," the monster said—it turned pinkish and looked modestly down at its claws— "I am quite peaceful. Pacific in nature. At heart, my dear boy, I assure you, I am gentle as a lamb."

Niko tried to ask a question. At first, no sound came out.

Then he said, in a high, strained voice, "But aren't you . . . a monster?"

"The designation," the creature said in an offended tone, "is highly rude."

Look what you've done, one part of Niko's mind shouted at him. *First you stumble into the monster. Then you have to insult it and make it angry.*

"Highly rude," the creature repeated huffily. "The proper, or common, name, as one might call it, is *drake* or *dragon*. We are, to be precise, a tridrake. A three-headed dragon. *Tri,* as in *trident, triangle,* and *tripod.*"

"I'm sorry," said Niko faintly. He gulped nervously. "But was it you that? . . . Have you ever? . . . Do you . . . eat sheep?"

"Eat sheep?" the dragon repeated. It shuffled its claws uncomfortably. "Well, I cannot deny, dear boy, that in the distant past I have—occasionally . . ." Its voice trailed off. "But not in recent centuries," it said firmly. "Dragons, by and large, are vegetarian. Besides"—it made a face—"sheep are so *woolly.* And they bleat."

"Vege . . . ?" Niko began uncertainly.

"We eat vegetables," the dragon said. "And cereal

30

grains and fruits." It eyed Niko severely. "Clearly, education is not what it used to be."

A breath of wind rustled the bushes, causing Niko to jump and look hastily over his shoulder.

The dragon looked with him.

"You seem on edge, dear boy," the dragon said. "A not uncommon state, I find, for humans. Perhaps a soothing soup . . ."

"There's a monster on the mountain," Niko said. His words tumbled over each other in his hurry to explain. "Everybody's frightened. Sheep have been disappearing for weeks—dragged off and killed. Just today, one of our lambs disappeared. And Jason—he lives in our village—*saw* the monster. He even saw its footprints. The monster ran along the ground and then the footprints just stopped. It vanished into thin air."

The dragon nodded.

"How big were these footprints?" it asked.

Niko shook his head. "Nobody saw them but Jason. It rained in the night and washed everything away. But he said they were *huge*. And he could see"—his eyes flickered uneasily toward the dragon's immense golden feet—"the marks where its claws dug into the ground."

The dragon hurriedly curled its golden claws out of sight.

"I see," it said unhappily. "I can only assure you, dear boy, that it was not me. That is, not I. I would never attack innocent ovines in such an uncivilized fashion. Decent dragons do not indulge in murderous theft."

Niko decided not to ask about the indecent dragons.

"I know that now," he said. "Now that I've talked to you. It was just . . . surprising . . . coming upon you so suddenly. I've never seen a dragon before. And you are . . . awfully large."

"Yes," the dragon agreed in pleased tones. It settled itself more comfortably in the grass.

"It has been a long time since I've had a really good conversation," it said wistfully. "Do tell me about yourself, dear boy. What do you do all day? And what do you want to do when you grow up? What is your favorite food? Your favorite color? And when is your birthday?"

In no time at all, Niko found himself talking to the dragon as if they were the oldest and best of friends. He learned that the dragon's favorite food was lemon pudding and that its favorite color was green; the dragon learned that Niko preferred pomegranates, fig cakes, and purple. Niko told the dragon about how he dreamed of going to Athens one day and of all the things he would like to learn. He asked the dragon its opinion of his plan to make a pair of giant feathered

wings, and the dragon replied with a somewhat con-
fusing story about the principles of aerodynamics.

As Niko and the dragon talked, evening fell.
The sky, Niko suddenly noticed, had grown dark. The
dragon glimmered before him, golden in the dimness.
Overhead, the stars were coming out. The two gazed
upward in companionable silence for a moment, lost
in the beauty of the night. The dragon gestured with
its golden tail.

"Magnificent," the dragon said. "Look carefully
and you should be able to see six thousand stars.
Dragons, of course," it continued in superior tones,
"can see many more. *We* have excellent eyesight."

Niko craned his neck back and studied the sky.
"People say," he said, "that the sky is a huge crystal
bowl set over the earth and the stars are stuck to the
inside of the bowl like little jewels."

"They do," the dragon said crisply. "People say
all sorts of things. Not all of them, unfortunately, are
correct."

Niko flopped over on his back and gazed up at
the stars with his mouth open.

"Beautiful, aren't they?" the dragon said. "Quite
jewel-like. But not jewels, dear boy, not at all. Think
about it."

Regretfully Niko scrambled to his feet.

"I wish we could talk more," he said. "But I have

to go home. It's late. I shouldn't have stayed so long. My mother and father will be terribly worried."

"Before you go," the dragon said, "I would check beneath the bush over there next to the big rock. I believe you will find what you came looking for."

Niko picked his way over to the bush. Beneath its branches lay Panno, sound asleep.

"He arrived some time before you did," the dragon said, "obviously confused. I'm sure he will be glad to return home."

Niko lifted the sleeping lamb. It was warm and heavy in his arm. Its curly fleece tickled his arms.

"Thank you," Niko said. "Thank you for everything."

"My pleasure, dear boy," the dragon said. It reached out one polished claw and patted Niko gently on the shoulder. "Have a safe journey home."

"Do come again," it added, "if you're ever up this way. I have enjoyed our visit."

"So have I," said Niko. "I'll think about what you said. About the stars, I mean."

"Do that," the dragon said. "Good night, dear boy."

Niko turned away and headed back down the mountainside.

6

THE MONSTER ON THE MOUNTAIN

Niko awoke the next morning when his little sister, Daphne, shook his arm. "Wake *up*, Niko," she kept repeating. Her small face was tear-stained and frightened. "Something terrible has happened," she said. "The monster came in the night." Tears rolled down her cheeks. "It came right into the village," she said. "It must have gone right past our house. It could get in anywhere. I'm scared."

Niko threw off his blanket, jumped to his feet, and pushed his hair back out of his eyes. "It will be all right, Daphne," he told her. "I'll go see what happened. No monster can get in here. You stay in the house and you'll be safe. Here, you can play with my toy horse." He handed her the little wooden horse on wheels that his father had made for him when he was a very little boy. It was one of Niko's treasures and Daphne always begged to hold it.

Leaving Daphne happily rolling the little horse back and forth across the floor, Niko ran outside. The entire village seemed to be standing in the street, shouting and yelling. Niko found his friend Stephanos at the edge of the crowd.

"What happened?" he asked. "What is everybody so upset about?"

Stephanos was a plump, cheerful boy with dark eyes and black hair. Usually he was full of jokes and laughter. Today he was solemn and pale. "The monster came right into the village," he told Niko. "Two houses were attacked in the night. The monster broke down fences and snatched sheep right out of the pens. Someone saw the creature through a window. A huge dark shape with eyes of fire." Stephanos shuddered.

A man's voice rose above the frightened babble of the crowd.

"We must hunt this monster down!" he bellowed. "We must band together and destroy it before it comes after our babies in their cradles and our children in their beds!"

"He's right!" shouted another. "We must kill the monster before it strikes again!"

"Arm yourselves!" yet another voice took up the cry. "Bring spears, daggers, bows! We will march together to the mountainside!"

People scattered to their homes and re-emerged carrying weapons. Peleus, the old carpenter, shouldered an immense iron ax. Zethus, the fisherman, hoisted a wickedly pointed spear. Diomedes, Niko's father, carried a curving wooden bow. Purposefully the men strode through the village toward the little track that headed to the sheep pastures and the higher reaches of the mountain.

"I'm going with them!" Stephanos shouted, racing after the marching men. "Come on, Niko! Come help kill the monster!" Niko saw that Stephanos wore a short dagger at his belt. Niko, too, started to run. When he reached the path heading to the sheep pastures, however, he ducked off to the right, away from the armed marchers. He wriggled through brambles and thicket, taking a shortcut toward the mountaintop. He climbed and ran, ran and climbed. He was panting for breath and there was a stitch in his side. Where had he been the night before? All the rocks and bushes looked suddenly alike. That rock shaped like a goat's head—had he seen that before?

"Dragon!" he shouted. "Where are you?"

There was a crackling sound of breaking branches, a sudden flash of gold.

37

"Right here, dear boy," the dragon's voice said.

Niko staggered through the bushes and sank to the ground.

The dragon was turned away from him. It appeared to be constructing something on a flat rock. Despite himself, Nikos was interested.

"What's that?" he panted.

"A primitive clock, dear boy," the dragon said. "A sundial. The shadow of the stick *here*"—it pointed—"falls on the marked dial *here* and tells the hour of the day."

Niko moved closer. "I see," he said. "The shadow moves as the sun moves."

The dragon shook his head. "No, no," it said. "Oh, no. The sun stands still. The *earth* moves."

Niko frowned, puzzled. "The *earth* moves?" he repeated in incredulous tones. "But everybody says . . ."

The dragon shook its head and held up a silencing claw. "Think about it," he said. "Observe. Weigh the evidence."

It peered at Nikos down the length of its golden nose.

"The scientific method," it said smugly.

Niko remembered his urgent errand. "Dragon," he said hastily, "I came to warn you. The monster attacked our village last night. It broke down fences

38

and killed sheep. Everyone is afraid that something even worse may happen next. All the men have taken their weapons and are on their way to search for the monster on the mountain. When they find it, they will kill it. And if they find you . . ."

"You feel they will assume the worst?" the dragon asked. "No time-out to assess the situation? No pause for clarification?"

"People are pretty upset," said Niko.

The dragon sadly shook its head. "Of course you are right," it said. "The time has come to seek more congenial climes. A pity. I have enjoyed my stay here. So restful. The urban architecture is superb. And such delicious olives."

It sighed. "And I enjoyed our little talk, dear boy. I had looked forward to getting to know you better."

"I'll never forget you, Dragon," Niko said.

The dragon bent its head low and looked deeply into Niko's eyes. It nodded rapidly several times. "You'll do very well," it said. "Very well indeed." For a moment, a golden claw gently stroked Niko's hair.

Then the dragon turned abruptly and moved back into the bushes.

"A few items to pack . . ." it said. "How long before your compatriots arrive?"

"Not very long at all," Niko said. "They were moving fast."

"Then farewell, dear boy," the dragon said. "You shouldn't be discovered here."

Niko nodded. "Goodbye," he said, one last time. Then he turned and headed rapidly back down the mountain.

To Niko's dismay, he found his eyes misted over, blinded by tears. He hated to see the golden dragon go. He stumbled over rocks and roots, tripped over branches. Finally his foot slipped off one jagged stone and he fell, sprawling full-length in the middle of the little path. He bumped his head and skinned both knees. Everything hurt. No one, Niko thought, could possibly be more miserable than he was at this very moment.

Then behind him he heard a sound that made the hair stand up on the back of his neck. A long, low, menacing growl. Very slowly Niko turned his head. His blood ran cold. There above him, straddling the path, stood a gigantic gray wolf. It bared its fangs, growling again deep in its throat. Stiff-legged, it took one step toward Niko, and then another.

This, Niko realized, horrified, was the villagers' monster. The real sheep-killer. And here he was weaponless, without even a knife to defend himself. Very slowly he stretched out his hand and gripped a stout stick. It was hopeless, he knew, but he couldn't just lie there, doing nothing, and let the wolf tear out his throat. At least he could die fighting. He gripped the stick tighter. The wolf crouched, snarling viciously, tensing its hind legs, preparing to spring.

Then it hesitated. Overhead, from the cloudless sky, came a sound of unexpected thunder. But this was not the rolling crash and rumble of a summer storm. This was the thunder of beating golden wings.

It was the dragon.

It roared into sight, blazing brilliant in the sun. As the wolf, recovering itself, sprang at Niko, the dragon swooped low and swung its glittering tail, catching the creature in mid-air. The wolf was flung across the mountainside. It crashed to the ground and lay still.

The dragon landed next to Niko, bending over him in concern.

"Are you all right, dear boy?" it asked.

Niko got shakily to his feet. He looked at the fallen body of the wolf and shuddered.

"It was a wolf," he said in a strangled voice. "A wolf. There wasn't a magical monster after all."

"Often there isn't," the dragon said. It, too, looked toward the fallen wolf. "A regrettable necessity," it said.

"It would have killed me," Niko said. "You saved my life."

"As you came to save mine," the dragon said.

Then, in a different voice, it said, "Please hold out your hand."

Puzzled, Niko put out his hand, palm upward. The dragon extended a long golden claw. Niko felt a sudden pang like a bee sting and then a lovely spreading warmth. There in the very center of his palm was a glittering fleck of gold.

"It is a sign," the dragon said. "The mark of the Dragon Friend. From this day on, dragons will know you and stand by you in time of trouble. As you have done for me."

Niko closed his hand tight over the precious mark.

From the distance they heard a clash of metal and the sound of shouting.

"That's the men from the village!" Niko cried. "Please, Dragon! You can't let them find you here!"

"Indeed," the dragon said. It spread its golden wings and rose slowly toward the sky. For a moment it hovered over the mountain path.

"Goodbye, dear boy," the dragon said. "And good luck."

By the time the first villagers burst through the trees, the dragon was lost in the distance. Only Niko, who was looking for it, could still see the last disappearing speck of gold.

Niko's father raced toward his son, calling his name. There was a confusion of voices and excited cries.

"What happened?"

"How did the boy come here?"

Then they discovered the body of the wolf.

Old Peleus approached it cautiously, ax raised. He prodded the wolf with one sandaled foot.

"Dead," he said.

"What happened?" someone else asked again. "Where's the monster?"

"It was a wolf," Niko said.

"What about the serpent's body and the lion's head?" someone shouted.

"And the wings and the flaming eyes?"

Jason, armed with a rusty sword, gingerly approached the dead wolf. He peered at it over old Peleus's shoulder. Then he began edging unobtrusively toward the back of the crowd.

"Niko has killed the wolf!" shouted Stephanos. "He's a hero!"

Niko started to protest. "No, I didn't," he said. "It wasn't me." But the villagers' voices drowned him out. No one heard him.

"Thank the gods you are not hurt," his father said, hugging him roughly. "I've never seen such a wolf. You should never have tried to battle the creature alone." He looked from the wolf to Niko and back again. "I am proud of you, my son."

"But . . ." Niko said.

"A hero!" shouted Stephanos again.

All the villagers began talking at once, laughing with relief. Old Peleus began to tell stories about wolves he had fought in his youth.

"It's all over now, son," Niko's father said. Then he raised his voice and said it louder. "It's all over. Let's go home."

Niko glanced up the the now-empty sky. The last glimmer of gold was gone.

"Yes," Niko said. "Let's go home."

J. P. King

The dragon fell silent. The three children roused themselves, stretching their legs on the cave floor.

"So what happened to Niko?" Zachary asked.

"He was never able to convince the villagers that he didn't kill the wolf," the dragon said. "No matter what he said, they insisted he was a hero."

"Well, he was," said Sarah Emily. "He saved you, didn't he? By warning you about the villagers in time? And he was going to fight the wolf with nothing but a stick. I think he was very brave."

The dragon nodded approvingly. "Others did too," it said. "Soon the story of his courage reached the ears of a rich local landowner. Such a fine boy, the landowner thought, should have an education. So he paid to send Niko to school in Athens. Niko did very well in school, though his teachers could never quite keep up with all his questions. When he grew up, he became an astronomer." The dragon gave a knowing little chuckle. "He was famed in his time for a crackpot hypothesis. He insisted that the earth was not the center of the universe. Instead, he said, the earth moves. It travels in circles around the sun."

Hannah had been silent, thinking.

Finally she said, "I don't know, Fafnyr. There wasn't any magical monster, but there *was* danger all the same. That wolf was dangerous. It almost killed Niko. Sometimes things that look scary aren't. Like you. But sometimes there's real danger. You have to be careful."

The dragon nodded ruefully. "Too true, my dear," it said. "But first you must observe and weigh the evidence."

It yawned widely. "The scientific method, you know," it said. The green eyes began to droop closed.

"We'd better be going," Zachary said.

"So delightful to see you," the dragon murmured. "Please return soon. My brother and sister will be most anxious for a visit."

Its eyes closed. There was a suspicion of a snore.

"Good night, Fafnyr," the children whispered. Zachary switched on the flashlight. Softly they turned and tiptoed quietly back toward the entrance of the cave. When they reached the ledge, they stood still for a moment, looking down at the blue ocean and the silent white boat.

"I'm confused," Sarah Emily said. "I don't think I understand Fafnyr's story. Was there a monster or wasn't there?"

Zachary was staring worriedly at the white yacht.

"I don't know," Hannah said. "It sounds like sometimes it's hard to tell."

When the children got back to the house, pink-cheeked and windblown from the hike from Drake's Hill, an excited Mrs. Jones met them at the kitchen door. She had been watching for them. "You'll never guess who's in your auntie's parlor," she said. "Mr. J.P. King, that's who. The man they call the Mystery Billionaire. He's been waiting for you for nearly half an hour."

"Who's that?" asked Sarah Emily. "I've never heard of him."

"*I* have," Zachary said. "He's really rich. He owns all these steel mills and things, and he's made about a zillion dollars in computers. He's in the newspapers all the time. Stories, no pictures. He won't have his picture taken ever."

"I've heard of him too," said Hannah. "He never goes out in public, and he lives on this enormous estate surrounded by high walls and security guards."

"He has houses all over the world," Zachary said. "In Paris and London and New York. And he owns this big ranch in Montana."

"Why is he *here*?" asked Hannah.

"He said he came to apologize," said Mrs. Jones. "He was passing by in his yacht and thought that the island was uninhabited. We told him that the island belongs to your auntie, who never allows visitors without her permission. Then he wanted to know who lives on the island, and we told him that it was just the two of us, and you three children, visiting. He said he was fond of children and would like to meet you. It's quite an honor. They say he never meets anybody."

Mrs. Jones smoothed her apron and bustled toward the refrigerator. "Just leave your jackets there on the chair and run along. I'll bring some tea—thank goodness Tobias bought lemons on his last trip to the mainland—and cocoa and fresh pound cake."

The children paused, flabbergasted, in the hall.

"J.P. King," Zachary whispered. *"Wow!"*

Together they stepped through the parlor door. There, sitting on a needlepoint chair and playing idly with Aunt Mehitabel's jade chess set, sat the man from the yacht. Now he was wearing khaki slacks and a blue sweater with a thin gold stripe across the chest. As the children entered the room, he got to his feet, smiled in a friendly manner, and held out his hand.

48

"The young explorers, I presume?" he asked. He shook hands with Hannah, then Zachary and Sarah Emily. "I am so pleased to meet you. My name is J.P. King. And you are? . . ."

"How do you do?" said Hannah politely. "I'm Hannah. This is my brother, Zachary, and my sister, Sarah Emily."

J.P. King resumed his seat and waved his hand hospitably toward Aunt Mehitabel's horsehair sofa.

"Do sit down and relax," he said, as if he were the host and the children the visitors.

The children perched on the edge of the sofa. The horsehair was slippery and uncomfortable, and the seat was so high that their feet dangled uncomfortably above the floor. Sarah Emily gripped the arm of the sofa to keep from sliding off.

"What a gift," Mr. King continued wistfully, "to live on this lovely and unusual island. While passing by in my yacht—perhaps you noticed my yacht, anchored offshore?—I was struck by its unspoiled natural beauty. I spend most of the year in the city—smog, traffic, litter, crowds. You have no idea how lucky you are."

"It's a perfectly beautiful boat," Hannah said. "Why doesn't it have a name?"

"Privacy, my dear," Mr. King said. "When one is as rich as I am—" He stopped, looking embarrassed. "Though my wealth is nothing compared to the riches you have here," he said quietly, gesturing at the window through which there was a view of rocky shoreline and blue bay.

There was a clatter of china in the hallway, and Mrs. Jones scurried in with a loaded tray of food. There was a steaming teapot, mugs of hot chocolate topped with whipped cream, a sliced pound cake, and a plate of oatmeal cookies. She set the tray on a low table in front of the sofa.

"Now, you children see to your guest," she said. "I'll make sure there's more hot water when you need some." She hurried away, staring back over her shoulder at Mr. King.

"Thank you," Mr. King said, accepting a cup of tea and a plate with a slice of pound cake. He took a bite. "Delicious."

"Mrs. Jones is a wonderful cook," Hannah said.

Mr. King leaned back in his chair, sipping his tea. He crossed his legs in his elegantly creased khaki slacks.

"I understand," he continued, "that the entire island is owned by your aunt?"

He set his teacup down, picked up one of the jade chess pieces, and began to turn it over and over in his fingers.

"Lovely," he said.

"Our great-great-aunt," Zachary said.

"She lives in Philadelphia," put in Hannah. "She doesn't allow visitors here."

Mr. King clamped his hand shut around the chess piece and gave an exclamation of dismay. "I didn't realize," he said. "I fear that—believing that the island was deserted, of course—I allowed some of my party to set up a small camp on the beach."

"I don't think Aunt Mehitabel would like that," Sarah Emily said. "She's a very private person."

Mr. King sighed. "I can understand wanting to keep this lovely place all to oneself," he said. "But perhaps when I see her—"

"I'm afraid that won't be possible," Hannah said. "She was planning to meet us on the island, but it turned out that she couldn't. She had a fall and broke her ankle."

"Indeed?" Mr. King said in a startled voice. "So there's no chance of our meeting?" Deliberately he replaced the chess piece on the board and lifted his cup for another sip of tea. He sounded oddly relieved.

"No," said Sarah Emily baldly.

"I believe I saw you children playing today," Mr. King said. "On the hill at the far end of the island. Mrs. Jones tells me it is called Drake's Hill? What an unusual name."

The children were silent.

"Do you spend much time there?" Mr. King continued. "It must have a marvelous view."

"We don't really go there very often," said Hannah.

"It's one of our favorite places," Sarah Emily said, at the same time.

Zachary hastily made a spluttering noise in his cocoa.

Mr. King appeared not to notice. He leaned forward and set down his teacup.

"There's an amazing population of wildlife on this island," he said. "Simply amazing. Why, just a few days ago I saw the most incredible sight. . . . Just take a guess. . . ."

Sarah Emily gave a tiny gasp.

Mr. King turned toward her inquiringly.

Hastily she shook her head. "I don't know," she said.

"Puffins!" Mr. King cried. "A flock of puffins! I wouldn't be surprised if they were nesting on the island."

"I've never seen any," Zachary said.

"Ah, well," Mr. King said.

He patted his lips with a napkin, folded it, and laid it carefully on his plate. "Simply delicious," he said. Then he got to his feet.

"I do hope we shall meet again soon," he said, giving the children another friendly smile. "I plan to write to your aunt to inform her of my presence here and will keep my yacht at anchor until I have a reply. Perhaps you three would like to come onboard for a visit?"

"On your *yacht*?" Hannah said excitedly.

Mr. King pulled a small leather notebook and a gold pencil from his pocket, scribbled something on a sheet of paper, tore it out, and handed it to Hannah.

"My personal telephone number," he said. "If you have time to arrange a visit, I can be reached here."

"It's been very nice meeting you," Hannah said.

Mr. King paused on the front porch, turning his head north and south, gazing the length of the island. He took a deep breath.

"Sea air," he said. "Open spaces. One gets the feeling that almost anything could happen here. Almost a magical place."

He gave a friendly nod, turned, and went down the porch steps. Beside the dock in the little cove, the children could see a small white motorboat floating.

"So that's how he gets to and from his yacht," Zachary muttered to Sarah Emily.

Mr. King lifted a hand in farewell. Then he walked quickly across the beach, stepped onto the dock, climbed into his motorboat, and sped away.

Zachary shut the front door and leaned against it.

"Whew," he said.

"I thought he was sort of nice," Hannah said. "I think you're just imagining things. He's really *famous*, Zachary."

"I wish he'd just go away," said Sarah Emily. "Him and his puffins."

"Well, he's not leaving," said Hannah. "You heard him. He's keeping his boat anchored here until he hears from Aunt Mehitabel. And I think we should give him the benefit of the doubt. Weigh the evidence, like Fafnyr said."

"I think we should warn Fafnyr," Sarah Emily said.

"*F*," Zachary said.

8

An Awful Warning

Sarah Emily was having a wonderful dream. She was flying, swooping and soaring high above the ocean in glorious loops and dips and glides. The air smelled clean and salty—she could smell it even in her dream—and there was a distant squawky sound of seagulls. Far below her the sea was a beautiful shade of cobalt blue, dotted with lacy froths of white where the waves were whipped by wind. She was over the island, she realized suddenly. There it was, Lonely Island, a crescent-shaped sliver of gray and green, surrounded by glittering sea. The sun glinted off the weathervane on the rooftop of Aunt Mehitabel's house, and then there was an answering glint from somewhere else, to the north, beyond the craggy tumble of rock that formed the hill. She flew toward it, curious. It came again, a silvery flash, as if someone were signaling with a mirror. She dived, dipping a powerful wing, and the sun blazed off her scales, blindingly golden . . .

She sat up, her heart beating fast. The sun was shining in her eyes and someone was pounding on her bedroom door.

"S.E.! Are you up?" It was Hannah's voice. "Zachary says he's found something. In the Tower Room."

The children thought that the Tower Room was the most wonderful room in Aunt Mehitabel's house. Its door was always kept locked, but last summer Aunt Mehitabel had sent them its strange little iron key.

Hannah opened Sarah Emily's bedroom door and peeked inside. She was barefoot and wearing lavender flannel pajamas.

"Come on," she said. "Don't bother to get dressed. Zachary said to hurry."

Together the girls scampered to the end of the hall and, one by one, climbed the narrow staircase that led to the third floor. At the top of the stairs, the door to the Tower Room stood ajar, the key, with its odd little curlicued handle, still in the lock. Behind the door was an iron ladder at the top of which was a trapdoor, now open. They climbed, one after the other, and scrambled out onto the tower floor.

They were in a small octagonal room, surrounded by round windows that looked like portholes. Zachary always felt that those windows must have made the sea captain who built the house feel as if he were back in his ship's cabin. Sarah Emily stood up and slowly looked around, breathing deeply through her nose. She loved the way the Tower Room smelled: like gingerbread and cedar chips, with a crinkly hint of mothballs and iodine. It made her think of hidden treasures and mysterious trunks stuffed with old satin ball gowns, peacock-feather fans, frock coats with gold buttons, and beaded dancing shoes.

The room was filled with a peculiar jumble of things. There were shelves of old books, their cracked leather bindings stamped in gold, a collection of rainbow-colored shells and odd-shaped stones, children's toys from long ago—some of them had once been Aunt Mehitabel's— and, on a carved stand, a brass gong with a little red wooden hammer hanging by a silk cord from its side.

Zachary was bending over something on the sea captain's desk, which was open, revealing all its rows of tiny drawers and pigeonholes. Zachary wanted to have a desk just like it when he grew up, with secret compartments and a glass inkwell, though Sarah Emily thought that, knowing Zachary, he'd need a place to put a computer too.

"What did you find?" Sarah Emily asked.

"It was in the bookcase," Zachary said. "I pulled out a book and it just fell out."

The book was still on the floor. Hannah picked it up.

"*A Historie of Magical Beastes,*" Hannah read. "*With Tales of Griffyns, Basilisks, Mermaids, Dragons, and an Account of the Marvelous Vegetable Lamb.* Published by Marlowe & Perkins, Ltd., London, 1727."

"It's not nearly as interesting as it sounds," said Zachary. "It's mostly in Latin and the pictures are all sort of smudgy. But look at this."

It was an old-fashioned black-and-white photograph. There were two women in it, both wearing straw hats with ribbons around the crowns and droopy long-waisted dresses. The taller of the two had a long pointed nose on which were perched a pair of spectacles. She looked cross. The shorter woman was laughing and squinting into the sun. Between them was a little boy in a sailor suit.

"Who are they?" Sarah Emily asked.

Zachary turned the photograph over and showed them the back.

"'Me, Anna, and Johann,'" he read, pointing. "And then this was written under it. It looks like it was added afterward."

Hannah leaned forward. "'*An Awful Warning,*'" she read slowly.

"I think it's Aunt Mehitabel's writing," Zachary said

"Why is it an Awful Warning?" Sarah Emily asked.

"And who are they?" asked Hannah. "Who are Anna and Johann? And who's Me?"

"Let's ask Aunt Mehitabel," Zachary said. "We should write her anyway. About J.P. King."

"Somebody's calling," Sarah Emily said.

It was Mrs. Jones, downstairs, sounding very faint and far away.

"She's saying 'pancakes,'" Sarah Emily said.

"Let's go eat," Zachary said. "We can write Aunt Mehitabel after breakfast."

9

An Unpleasant Encounter

After Mrs. Jones's blueberry pancakes were finished—
Zachary had eaten eight, with lots of maple syrup—and
the dishes finished and the letter to Aunt Mehitabel
written, the children prepared to hurry back to Drake's
Hill.

"Read it one more time," Sarah Emily said. "Just to
make sure we remembered everything."

The letter was printed on Hannah's best stationery,
which was lavender with a border of purple pansies.

"Dear Aunt Mehitabel," Hannah read.

> *"We all hope your ankle is feeling better. F
> is fine, but there are some strangers on the island.
> Mr. J.P. King arrived in his yacht and has put up
> a camp on the beach. We told him that the*

island is private, but he won't leave until he hears
from you.

And one other thing. We found a picture stuck
in a book in the Tower Room. The picture says Me,
Anna, and Johann *on the back, and then there's a*
note that says An Awful Warning. *Who are the*
people in the picture? And why is it an Awful
Warning?

Please write back soon.

Love from Hannah, Zachary, and Sarah Emily

"It's fine," Zachary said, busily stuffing granola bars,
apples, and plastic bottles of lemonade into his backpack.

Hannah folded the letter, put it in a lavender envelope, sealed it, and stuck on a stamp.

"You can't be packing *food,*" she said in tones of hor-
ror. "Not after all those pancakes. I'm so stuffed, I don't
think I ever want to eat again."

"They were *small* pancakes," Zachary said.

"They were not," said Hannah.

Zachary ignored her. "Let's get going," he said.

They set off briskly, walking fast, eager to get back to
the dragon's cave. By the time they reached the foot of
Drake's Hill, the sun was high overhead. The sky was a
clear deep blue, and the air smelled cleanly of the distant ocean. Nothing, it seemed, should go wrong on
such a perfect morning.

"Let's go check the camp," Zachary said. "Before we go to the cave. Let's just see if they're still there."

They were.

In the center of the cluster of white tents, next to a ring of rocks that had once held a campfire, was a group of people. There were several young men all dressed alike in what looked like uniforms: navy-blue pants and white windbreakers with name tags on the breast pockets. There was also a girl wearing a rubber wetsuit. She held a diving mask and a pair of rubber flippers in one hand, and there were air tanks in a harness on the ground next to her feet.

They seemed to be getting orders. A man with a clipboard was talking rapidly, pointing at each person in turn, and then making check marks on the clipboard with a pencil.

"I wish we could hear what they're saying," Hannah whispered in a frustrated voice.

Zachary gave a little exclamation and began to rummage in the backpack. He pulled out his tape recorder and microphone.

"We can," he whispered excitedly. He switched on the tape recorder. "We just have to plant the microphone somewhere closer—it's got a really long cord—and then we'll be able to hear every word they say. You two stay here. I'll be right back."

Holding the tiny microphone, he crawled rapidly to the edge of the sheltering fir trees and tossed the tiny microphone toward the speakers. It fell invisibly into a clump of beach grass. Zachary scooted quickly backward to where Hannah and Sarah Emily waited.

"Now listen to this," he said. He switched the tape recorder on.

". . . underwater caves," a scratchy voice said. "Mr. King seems to think there might be something of interest along this stretch of beach. That will be your job, Alison. Take Danny along to stand watch while you dive."

There was an inaudible murmur that sounded like Alison asking a question.

"No, just caves," the scratchy voice said. "See what's in them. And Mike and Tony, you two head down the beach and see if you can spot anything else in the way of rock formations. And Ben can cover the hill."

"Not *again*," somebody—presumably Ben—said in tones of disgust. "I've been over every inch of that blasted rock pile."

"Not quite," the scratchy voice said. "Mr. King wants complete maps of the terrain—you haven't delivered those yet—and detailed notes on the resident wildlife. And I might add, Ben, that if you're interested in keeping your job, you'll have to do better than one misspelled note reading 'Saw a dum raccoon.'"

Ben snorted.

"All right, then," the scratchy voice said. "Let's get going. Report back here by five o'clock and we'll compare notes."

There was a confused mutter of voices as the group began to scatter, talking among themselves.

Zachary turned the little tape recorder off.

"Well, that's that," he said. "They're looking for something all right."

"Zachary," Sarah Emily said urgently. "That man . . ."

A man in a white windbreaker was just straightening up from the clump of beach grass, a puzzled expression on his face. In one hand he was holding Zachary's microphone.

"Quick!" Hannah hissed. "We've got to get out of here!"

Zachary yanked on the cord, struggling to unplug the microphone from the tape recorder. At the same time, the man in the windbreaker began to run toward the trees, following the telltale path of the cord.

"What the devil do you think you're doing?" he shouted as the children scrambled to their feet. "Who are you, anyway?"

He had broad shoulders, short reddish hair, and a narrow sullen-looking face. The name tag on his pocket read BEN. He gave a vicious tug on the microphone cord, and the tape recorder flew out of Zachary's hands and landed with a crunching noise on the ground.

Zachary, red-faced, bent to pick it up. Sarah Emily had turned pale.

"We're studying birdcalls," Hannah said, with great presence of mind. She put one arm around Sarah Emily. "For a school project."

Zachary, whose mouth had fallen open, abruptly closed it and tried to look like a bird-lover.

"There was a sandpiper," Hannah went on, looking up at the man with wide innocent eyes. It was an expression that often worked well on strangers but never fooled her family. Ben didn't seem to be fooled either. He must have been smarter than he looked.

"I didn't see any sandpiper," he said suspiciously. "I think you kids better come with me. Mr. King, he doesn't like people snooping around."

"This is our aunt's island, not his," Zachary said boldly. "If anybody's snooping, it's you. We're not going anywhere with you."

"We'll see about that," Ben said. He lunged forward, grabbed Zachary roughly by the upper arm, and yanked. Zachary, pulled off-balance, staggered forward. "Come on, all three of you. Move it."

"Leave him *alone!*" Hannah cried. She grabbed Zachary's other arm.

"What is all this?" a new voice said.

It was the elderly Chinese man they had seen coming out of the tent on the previous morning. He was still wearing his black suit and embroidered cap. Now that he was so close to them, the children could see that the cap was patterned with scarlet birds, gold flowers, and a wriggly sort of turquoise creature that might have been a winged serpent. He looked very tall and menacing standing there beneath the trees. His skin was the color of old ivory and his mouth was folded tightly shut in a thin slash like a knife cut. Beside her, Hannah could feel Sarah Emily shiver.

"Just kids snooping around, Mr. Chang," the man named Ben said.

"Let the boy go, Ben," Mr. Chang said. "Let them go." He had a dry whispery voice that reminded Hannah of rustling paper. "They are nothing to worry about. Go about your business."

Ben shambled off through the trees, looking resentfully backward over his shoulder. Mr. Chang pointed his finger threateningly at the children.

"Now leave!" Mr. Chang said. "And do not return!"

The children turned and ran.

They crept cautiously along the shelf of rock leading to the broad platform before the cave.

"Crawl," Zachary said tensely. "Mr. King might be out on the deck with his binoculars. Looking for *puffins*. Or that Ben may be sneaking around."

They scuttled across the ledge on hands and knees. From behind a sheltering rock, they peered down at the floating yacht. The deck was deserted.

Zachary heaved a sigh of relief. Then he gave a little gasp of dismay and pointed to the rocks below.

"Something fishy's going on," he said unhappily. "Look at that."

A figure in a white windbreaker was working its way along the steep face of the hill, feeling at cracks and crevices, pausing every now and then to tap at the rock with a geologist's hammer.

Sarah Emily drew a shaky breath. "I'm scared," she said.

"Let's go see Fafnyr," Hannah said. "Right now, before anything else happens."

The three children ducked quickly into the cave. Again, all was suddenly quiet and dark, the crashing roar of the waves gone utterly still. Zachary switched on his flashlight and the children edged their way inward and down, breathing in the tangy odor of smoke and cinnamon—the now-comforting smell of dragon. A streak of gold flashed in the gloom. Zachary's flashlight had picked up the glitter of dragon scales.

There was a soft hiss as the dragon flamed, and the cave glowed with light. This time the second head was awake. Cool blue eyes surveyed the children. The dragon's voice was deep and husky. "Hannah, Zachary, Sarah

Emily," the dragon began. "I am inexpressibly delighted to see you once again."

Then its voice changed and it bent its neck to study the children more closely.

"Something has happened," said the dragon in a concerned voice.

The children sank down on the cave floor, leaning back against the dragon's warm golden tail.

"We met some people on the beach," Sarah Emily said.

"They're poking all over the island," Hannah said. "Looking for caves. We were trying to find out what they were doing, but one of them caught us. He grabbed Zachary and yanked him around."

"The mannerless cad," the dragon said.

"They all work for Mr. King," said Zachary. "And he's written to Aunt Mehitabel, asking for permission to stay on the island."

"He's *dangerous*," Sarah Emily said. She looked from the dragon to her brother and sister. "I just know he's trying to find out about Fafnyr."

"But how can he *possibly* know anything about Fafnyr?" Hannah said. "Besides, Aunt Mehitabel will tell him to go away."

"What if he doesn't pay any attention to her?" asked Zachary. "She's in Philadelphia, with a broken ankle. She can't really do anything. What if he sticks around anyway? How are we going to stop him?"

"We could fight them," said Sarah Emily doubtfully.

"That's easy to *say*," said Zachary. "We're just kids. And anyway I hate fighting. There are a couple of kids at school who always want to fight, just to see who's bigger or better. If I don't fight, they laugh and call names and say I'm a chicken. I'm not a chicken. I just think fighting is stupid."

The dragon nodded sympathetically.

"Battle," it said, "is a highly overrated activity." The blue eyes took on a dreamy, faraway look. "That reminds me of a story," the dragon said. "A tale of chivalry and honor. Perhaps you would like to hear it?"

"Knights and castles," said Sarah Emily excitedly. "I love those stories. I've been reading all about King Arthur and Sir Lancelot and Guinevere. And the sword in the stone."

"Fighting," said Zachary glumly.

The dragon reached out a polished golden claw and smoothed his hair.

"There's fighting and there's fighting," it said. "Just listen."

The dragon began to speak. As the children listened to its voice, the walls of the cave again seemed to fade. They heard a sudden triumphant flourish of trumpets, the sound of clashing metal, and a thunder of galloping horses' hooves. Then there came the soft strum of a lute, a chatter of voices and laughter, and a wonderful aroma of baked apples and roasting meat. The children once again were in another place and another time.

The Blue-Eyed Dragon's Story
GAWAIN AND ELEANOR

"Gawain," the dragon said, "was eleven years old and a page. He had come to Hampton Castle when he was just seven, sent by his father and mother to learn courtly manners and the arts of battle, under the tutelage of the owners of the castle, Lord Charles and Lady Margaret. He spent his days practicing the use of weapons, perfecting his horseback-riding skills, and learning to polish and repair armor. In the evenings, he waited upon the lord and lady and their household as they ate their dinner. Gawain was in training to become a knight. But sometimes knighthood seemed very far away. . . ."

Gawain sat on a step in the doorway of the castle kitchen, kicking his heels, waiting until it was his turn to help serve the guests at the banquet in progress in the Great Hall. Behind him, the cook and his helpers were working furiously, preparing platter after platter of food. Servants swept by carrying roast boars with apples in their mouths, whole peacocks, gilded and trimmed with their own green-and-blue tail feathers, and an elaborate sweet in the form of an enormous galleon with spread sails made of sugar.

Gawain was bored. He hated being a page. He dreamed of the days when he would be a knight, dressed in flashing armor and a helmet topped with flowing plumes, riding off on a white charger to battle the enemy with sword, lance, and shield. He wanted to be like Sir Tristram, oldest son of Lord Charles. Sir Tristram, in Gawain's opinion, was everything a knight should be: wonderfully handsome, unfailingly courteous, and gloriously brave.

"Gawain!" someone shouted from the kitchen. "More wine! Look alive, lad!" Then there was a startled shriek and a crash of falling crockery.

"*Gawain!*" the voice shouted again, louder.

Gawain sighed and rose from his seat. In the kitchen, he stepped around a puddle of spilled gravy on the flagstone floor, then filled a pitcher with wine and carried it carefully to the Great Hall. There, moving

71

quietly behind the guests, he filled each empty goblet. Then he went to stand patiently at Lord Charles's right elbow, awaiting any instructions from the lord or his lady. As the company ate and drank, a troubador dressed in green velvet stepped forward, strummed upon a lute, and began to sing a song of many verses, all about gallant deeds of war.

Gawain shifted restlessly from foot to foot, rustling the clean straw scattered with rose petals that was strewn on the hall floor. His gaze swept around the high stone walls, hung with crossed lances, swords, shields, and silk-embroidered banners. "Sir Gawain," he whispered under his breath. His fingers drummed on the wine pitcher. He was very bored.

Only one other person in the castle was as bored and unhappy as Gawain. That was his best friend, Eleanor. Eleanor was ten, the very youngest of Lady Margaret's ladies-in-waiting. Her parents had sent her to Hampton Castle to learn all the graces of noble ladies. She was to learn to dance and sing, to play upon the lute, and to master the art of fine embroidery so that she could make exquisite tapestries. Eleanor was a poor pupil. She hated it all.

"I will never be a lady," she told Gawain in despair as they stood on the castle wall, looking out toward the great green forest and the distant blue hills.

"Everything I do is wrong. I fall over my own feet when I dance the galliard. I can't carry a tune. I hate embroidery. All my stitches are crooked, and I keep pricking my fingers. My unicorns look like pigs."

Gawain made a sympathetic sound. He didn't know what to say. After all, there wasn't much else for a girl to do.

"Nobody even talks about anything interesting," Eleanor went on. "All the ladies-in-waiting talk of nothing but fashions and face paint and the best way to dress their hair. And Sir Tristram." She put her chin in the air, batted her eyelashes very fast, and imitated someone else's voice. "He's *so* handsome!" she said. "*So* powerful! And *such* golden hair!" She resumed her own voice. "He's a conceited dolt. He has absolutely no conversation. He talks of nothing but his sword and his stupid horse."

Gawain was shocked. "He's a perfect knight, Eleanor," he said. "Perfect. He won every joust in the tournament last year. I want to be just like him someday."

Eleanor snorted through her nose. "I certainly hope not," she said.

Two days after the banquet, Eleanor brought Gawain some interesting news. A wandering minstrel had stopped by the castle, hoping to earn a few pennies with his songs.

"All rags and patches, poor thing," said Eleanor, "with a pet squirrel on his shoulder. The squirrel would take nuts right out of your hands. And he sang beautifully."

"The squirrel?" asked Gawain.

Eleanor poked him in the ribs. "No, not the squirrel. The minstrel," she said. "And he told us"—she paused impressively—"that a dragon has been sighted in the southern part of the forest."

"A real dragon?" exclaimed Gawain. "I thought they were only in the old tales."

"No," said Eleanor smartly. "A stuffed dragon. What is wrong with you today? Of course a real dragon. Whoever finds the beast and slays it will be a hero. Everybody is talking about it. Sir Tristram is having his armor refurbished, and the castle blacksmith is sharpening his sword."

Gawain kicked a cobblestone viciously with one red leather shoe. "I hate being a page," he grumbled. "I wish I were Sir Tristram, riding out to battle the dragon. It's not fair."

Eleanor brushed dust from the skirt of her blue gown.

"Well, why don't you?" she asked.

Gawain glared at her. "Because I'm not a knight," he said in an exaggeratedly patient tone of voice. "Because I don't have a horse. Or armor. Or a sword."

"If you slay the dragon," said Eleanor, "it would be a great deed and Lord Charles would make you a knight. You would have a suit of armor and a silk banner all your own. You could have a dragon on it. They would call you Gawain the Dragon-Slayer. You'd have everything you've been waiting for."

"But how?" said Gawain. "I can't kill a dragon with my bare hands. Or a slingshot. That's all I've got."

"There are swords in the castle armory," said Eleanor. "All kinds of swords. You could borrow one."

"That's stealing," said Gawain.

"Not if you put it back afterward," said Eleanor. "You get the sword and meet me by the back gate at midnight. Then we'll find the dragon."

Gawain shook his head. "You can't go, Eleanor," he said. "A true knight would never let a lady go on a dragon quest. You're supposed to give me a favor—a handkerchief or a hair ribbon or something—and then wait for me to come back with the dragon's head."

Eleanor looked stubborn. "If you don't let me go with you," she said, "I won't tell you which road to take through the wood. You'll never find the dragon if you go alone. So you might as well give in."

Gawain argued, but Eleanor refused to budge. At last it was agreed that the children would go together—provided, Gawain insisted, that Eleanor promised to stand back out of the way when the fighting began.

"I'll embroider a tapestry for you when it's all over," Eleanor called over her shoulder as she hurried back to the ladies' solar. "If you don't mind having your dragon look a bit like a cow."

That night Gawain lay on his pallet with the other pages in the anteroom of Lord Charles's bed-chamber. He was afraid to fall asleep. If I do, he thought to himself, I might sleep right past midnight. Then Sir Tristram will find the dragon first and kill it before I do, and I will never be a hero.

He reached under the pallet to feel the hidden sword. He had sneaked it out of the castle armory that afternoon, concealing it under his cloak. It was a fine straight sword with a good balance, not too heavy, the hilt engraved with a pattern of silver leaves. There was a leather scabbard to go with it and a belt with a silver buckle.

At last Gawain judged that it must be midnight. The castle was asleep. He could hear muffled snores from the room next door, where Lord Charles and Lady Margaret slept in a carved bed hung with red velvet curtains. An owl hooted outside the window. Softly, trying not to rustle the pallet's straw stuffing, Gawain got to his feet. He wrapped himself in his cloak, slipped on his shoes, and picked up the sword.

Quietly he crept out of the room and down the stone stairs.

Eleanor was waiting for him by the back gate. She held a lantern in one hand, hiding its light with a fold of her hooded cloak. They slid back the bolts on the gate. The iron made a horrid screeching sound, and Gawain and Eleanor held their breath, waiting for someone to shout, "Who's there?" But all remained quiet. Silently they opened the heavy wooden door, passed through it, and set out on the road to the forest.

11

THE DRAGON QUEST

"This is it," Eleanor said. The lantern, with its single lighted candle, shone dimly on a narrow leafy trail. "The second path to the right off the south road. That's what the minstrel said."

"Are you sure?" Gawain asked. He peered doubtfully into the trees. "It doesn't look as if anything has passed this way in years."

"It's exactly what he said," Eleanor said firmly. "I have a very good memory."

She lifted the lantern and stepped forward onto the trail, her cloak sweeping the branches. Gawain followed. The little path wandered endlessly through the forest, twisting between bushes and trees. They walked for what seemed like miles and miles. The night began to fade, from dark to dimness, from black to pale gray. Then the sun rose and a faint light began to glimmer through the leaves. Eleanor blew the stub of the candle out.

"My feet are tired," she said.

"This trail is leading nowhere," said Gawain. "I don't think your minstrel knew what he was talking about. Him and his squirrel. And I'm thirsty. Do you hear running water?"

Just off the path to the left was a clear trickling stream. Both children bent to drink. The water was cold and sweet. The ends of Eleanor's braids dipped in it and dripped on the grass.

Gawain sat back, dropping the sword at his side.

"Should we keep going?" he asked. "Or turn around and go back to the castle?"

Eleanor squeezed the water out of her hair. Then suddenly she caught her breath. "Look!" she said, pointing.

There, in the soft ground on the other side of the stream, was the print of a great clawed foot.

"A dragon footprint!" Gawain whispered. "And it's fresh. It must be very near."

They crossed the stream, balancing on a fallen tree trunk, and ran to the site of the footprint, crouching down to examine it more closely.

"It must have stopped for a drink," Gawain said. "Just like we did."

"There's another print," said Eleanor, pointing.

"Broken branches," said Gawain. "It went this way. Come on. Stay behind me."

They pushed their way through the underbrush, following the trail of tracks, crushed grass, and broken branches. Eleanor's skirt tangled in the brambles, and Gawain's sword kept banging against the trunks of trees. At last, almost between one step and another, they stumbled out of the woods and into a wide grassy clearing.

There before them, flashing gold in the morning sun, stood the dragon.

It was much larger and more frightening than Gawain or Eleanor had expected. It had a long heavy arrow-pointed tail, smooth golden wings folded over its gleaming back, and three heads. One head, angrily awake, was glaring directly at the children. Its eyes were a piercing blue. The other two heads were curled low on the dragon's shoulders. They seemed to be fast asleep.

Gawain's legs felt as if they were made out of soft putty. His mouth was dry with fear. But he wanted to win his knighthood, and he knew it was up to him to protect Eleanor. He drew his borrowed sword—it looked much smaller and flimsier now than it had in the castle armory—and stepped bravely forward.

"Dragon!" he shouted in a voice that sounded wobbly and strange. "Dragon! Prepare to meet thy doom!"

The dragon snorted. It sounded crusty and annoyed.

Eleanor, behind him, gave a little shriek. "Gawain!" she shouted. "Look out! Dragons can breathe fire!"

But the dragon breathed out no incinerating flames. Instead, as Gawain ran forward, sword held high, it swung out its tail with a quick twist. The sword catapulted out of Gawain's hand and soared high into the air, tumbling end over end, and finally plummeted into the center of a blackberry thicket. Gawain looked after it in dismay.

"For heaven's sake, young man," the dragon snapped. "Whatever is the matter with you? No breakfast? Got up on the wrong side of the bed?"

The dragon lowered its head so that it could look Gawain directly in the eye.

"Time hanging heavy on your hands, so you decided to try a spot of murder and mayhem?"

Gawain heard Eleanor's voice behind him. It shook a little.

"You . . . you can talk," she said.

"What did you expect?" the dragon asked sarcastically. "Grunts? Moos? Twitters? Mindless babble?"

Eleanor stepped forward to stand beside Gawain. "I don't know," she said. "I didn't think."

"Humans seldom do," the dragon said in a disgusted voice.

"Well, everyone knows what dragons are like," Gawain spoke up defensively. "Gallant knights are always fighting them in all the legends. Look at the story of the dragon and Saint George."

"*Saint George*," the dragon repeated coldly. "A hoodlum. A brain like a pea."

"And what about the princesses?" Gawain said. "Dragons are always kidnapping princesses."

"Not any dragon *I* know," the dragon said. "What would a dragon want with a princess? They're dull creatures. They whine. They wear silly shoes."

It raised one golden claw and made a twirly motion in the region of its ear.

"And they're always fussing with their hair," it said.

Eleanor shot Gawain a triumphant look. "I told you so," she said.

The dragon waved its claw in an admonishing fashion.

"A dragon," it said, "is polite and considerate. Tolerant, unassuming, and impeccable in the matter of personal hygiene. Brave and industrious, gentle and modest . . ."

At that moment, there was a loud sound of crashing in the bushes and the noise of pounding hooves. Into the clearing burst Sir Tristram, mounted on his white charger. He looked magnificent. His armor glinted in the sun; the scarlet plumes on his helmet fluttered in the wind. His sword was drawn and waving overhead.

"Dragon!" Sir Tristram bellowed. "Prepare to die!"

The dragon briefly rolled its eyes heavenward. "Not twice in one morning," it muttered. Again it lifted its golden tail and swung it neatly to one side. It knocked Sir Tristram off his horse. The white charger came to an abrupt halt and, after one horrified look at the dragon, turned tail and galloped rapidly off the way that it had come. Sir Tristram landed with a jangle of clashing metal. He tripped, stumbled, tried to recover his balance, and fell clumsily on his own sword. The blade pierced his thigh between the heavy plates of armor. He gave a howl of outrage and pain.

Gawain and Eleanor rushed to help him as he struggled to get to his feet. Blood dripped into the grass.

"Villain!" Sir Tristram was shouting at the dragon. "Unprincipled beast! Pewling blackguard! Monster!"

"Oaf," the dragon snapped back. "Bully. It serves you right."

Then, ignoring the knight's furious bellows, it turned to the children. "I suppose I cannot in good conscience let the idiot bleed to death," it said. "Help him out of that ridiculous metal suit."

Sir Tristram sank back down on the ground. Eleanor pulled off his helmet. His face had gone pale. The children helped him stretch out in the grass and wrestled to undo the buckles and straps that held on his armor. The wound was a deep slash in his right thigh. It looked painful.

"Wash it with clean water," the dragon directed. "Then pack the wound with old moldy bread—there's some in that basket—and wrap the leg in bandages."

"*Moldy bread?*" repeated Eleanor.

"I bake," the dragon said. "Whole wheat."

"That can't be right," Eleanor said. "Moldy bread? That awful blue stuff? It might kill him."

The dragon sighed and shook its head. "That blue-green fuzz that you humans have been so foolishly throwing away," it said pompously, "is a most valuable organism. Eventually one of you will doubtless figure out that it produces a disease-combating substance."

"Just do what it says," Gawain whispered. "It seems to know what it's doing."

"I do," the dragon said. It glared at Gawain down the length of its golden nose.

Obediently Eleanor found the basket and packed Sir Tristram's wound with moldy bread. Then she tore her cloak into long strips and wrapped the leg gently in cloth bandages. Gawain brought Sir Tristram a drink of cold water, carried in his helmet. The knight drank thirstily. Then he lay back in the grass and closed his eyes.

Gawain and Eleanor sat down beside him. Gawain, for the first time, glanced around the clearing. At one end, there was a lean-to built of sticks. It contained several baskets, a table made of stacked flat stones, and an assortment of leafy plants in pots.

Gawain turned to the dragon. "Do you live here?" he asked.

"Not permanently, young man," the dragon said. "And just as well," it said. It looked pointedly at Sir Tristram. "I was attempting to commune with nature. I was camping."

Gawain looked puzzled.

"I was *trying*," the dragon said plaintively, "to escape from the stresses of modern life."

Eleanor sighed. "What do we do now?" she said. She gestured toward Sir Tristram, now soundly asleep with his mouth open. "We can't get him home," she said.

"You will have to stay here until he heals," the dragon said in resigned tones. "In two weeks or so, barring any other unexpected visits."

Then it said more cheerfully, "We will have an exciting time. You can tell me all about yourselves. And I will teach you to bake."

12

THE HEALERS

Gawain and Eleanor spent two weeks in the forest with the dragon. They went on nature walks, picked berries, fished, and told stories and sang songs around nightly campfires. The dragon taught both children to bake a respectable loaf of bread, though some of their earlier efforts went dreadfully wrong. Gawain built a simple catapult that they used to fling the blackened failures at a target pinned to a tree. The dragon enjoyed this, and once burned an entire batch of muffins to provide them with more ammunition.

Sir Tristram's leg grew stronger every day until finally he was ready to return to the castle. His warhorse, looking sheepish, had come back to the clearing. Sir Tristram mounted cautiously. His sword and armor were tied in a neat bundle behind him on the saddle. He thanked the dragon and the children politely for their care. He planned to leave immediately on a crusade, where he hoped to regain his self-respect. He invited Gawain to go with him as his squire, but Gawain only shook his head.

The dragon looked downcast as the knight galloped away.

"A crusade," it said, in tones of contempt. "They never learn." It heaved a discouraged sigh, staring into the forest in the direction Sir Tristram had gone.

"Thick as a post," it said.

Eleanor turned to Gawain. "What did I tell you?" she said.

The dragon, too, turned its blue gaze toward Gawain. "And you?" it said. "You didn't seem eager to accompany him. I thought your fondest wish was to be a knight, galloping off to battle."

Gawain looked down and shook his head.

"I always thought fighting looked so glorious," he said. "I wanted to be a hero." He looked at his feet. "I wanted to slay a dragon too. But it all looks different when you think about the other side."

He sighed. "Now I don't know what I want to do."

The dragon patted him kindly on the shoulder with a polished golden claw. "There are heroes and there are heroes," it said. "You'll think of something. You both will. Don't worry about that."

It paused for a moment, gazing solemnly into their eyes.

"It's not fighting that's so difficult," the dragon finally said. "It's deciding what's worth fighting *for*."

The children shifted on the cave floor and stretched their arms and legs. It felt as though they hadn't moved for a long time. The dragon's voice had ceased.

"Then what happened?" Zachary asked. "Did Gawain ever become a knight?"

"No," the dragon said. "He changed his mind after his stay in the forest. Instead, he and his wife became great healers, physicians. Between them they saved many lives."

"Who did he marry?" asked Sarah Emily.

"Eleanor, of course," said the dragon. "They were quite made for each other, those two. She never could manage embroidery, but she had a fine hand for surgery."

"What about Sir Tristram?" asked Hannah.

The dragon gave a chortling little snort. "He rode off on a crusade," it said, "and was captured in the

89

middle of his second battle. He was sold into slavery in Baghdad and ended up marrying the youngest daughter of the household. Her name was Zenobia. They had four daughters and Sir Tristram became a date merchant."

"A *date merchant*," said Sarah Emily in dismay. "That's not very romantic. It's not like the Round Table stories at all."

"Poor Sir Tristram," said Hannah.

"Oh, I don't know," the dragon said. "Perhaps after the bloodshed of the crusade, fighting didn't look so glorious to him either anymore. Perhaps at last he began to use his head. I like to think I may have had a hand in bringing him to his senses."

The dragon gave what might have been a little giggle. "Four daughters," it repeated. "And every one of them could wrap him right around her littlest finger . . ."

Sarah Emily was staring at the gleaming golden fleck in the center of her right palm.

"Did they become Dragon Friends?" she asked suddenly. "Gawain and Eleanor?"

The dragon nodded solemnly.

"Of course," it said. "I was honored."

Zachary said musingly, "What's worth fighting for . . ."

"Lives," said Sarah Emily suddenly. "That's it, isn't it, Fafnyr? All those people's lives—babies and sick people. That's what Gawain and Eleanor decided was worth fighting for."

For an instant, the dragon's eyes glowed a deeper, brighter blue. Then it settled down on the cave floor and gave an enormous yawn.

Hastily, Hannah brought up the problem of Mr. King. "The man on the yacht, Fafnyr. Mr. J.P. King. Do you know why he's so determined to keep hanging around? Did he see something?"

The dragon's gold turned faintly pink. "I fear I may have been a trifle careless," it mumbled. "I slipped out for a bit of exercise and a snack—*quite* early in the morning," it said indignantly, "*well* before he had any business being up, and there he was, pacing about on the deck of that overblown boat. He was looking into the sun, so I hoped he was confused about what he saw."

"We were afraid he'd seen you," Zachary said.

"Not *well,*" the dragon said. "Not in all that glare. And if nothing else happens, he'll decide that it was all his imagination and he'll leave. It's happened before. People are notoriously reluctant to believe."

"This time, I hope so," said Hannah.

"I don't know," said Zachary worriedly. "Mr. King never gives up on anything. At least, that's what the newspapers say. That's why he's so successful."

The dragon yawned again and the blue eyes began to droop. "I will, of course, consider this problem," the dragon murmured. "A bit later. After my nap." Its eyes closed farther.

"Do come again soon," it said. "My sister is anxious to see you."

"Good night, Fafnyr," Sarah Emily said. The only answer was a snore. The cave had gone dark.

Zachary switched on the flashlight, and the children picked their way carefully back to the cave entrance. As they emerged, blinking, from the cave into the spring sunlight, they looked down into the blue ocean, where, far below them, the white yacht still floated, rocking gently up and down on the waves.

"He seemed like such a nice man," Hannah said regretfully.

"He's a technological genius," Zachary said. "Everybody says so."

"Genius shmenius," said Hannah.

"I knew there was something funny about those puffins," Zachary said.

Sarah Emily said, "I wish we'd hear from Aunt Mehitabel."

✍ 13 ✍

A Difficult Proposal

A letter in burnt-orange ink, filled with exclamation points and underlinings, arrived from Aunt Mehitabel:

> *Dear Children,*
>
> *I have received a letter from Mr. J.P. King, announcing that he has been <u>lurking</u> off the north shore of the island in his yacht and would now like permission to land and <u>explore Drake's Hill</u>! I have written back, explaining that <u>under no circumstances</u> do I <u>ever</u> allow uninvited visitors on the island! I trust he will not risk trespassing again! He sounds a <u>most</u> determined person, <u>much</u> too accustomed to getting his own way.*
>
> *The Anna of the photograph that you found in the Tower Room—I had thought it was <u>long gone</u>—*

is Anna König, a woman who gr<u>ossly</u> deceived me and who, due to my foolishness, could have been a <u>terrible</u> threat to F! I met Anna long ago on a tour of archaeological sites in China. We both had a deep interest in dragon artifacts—mine, of course, because of you-know-who—and we soon became bosom friends. I even invited her to join me on Lonely Island, along with her son, Johann Pieter, a bright young boy of ten. The photograph that you describe is of the three of us, taken at the beginning of that <u>fatal</u> visit.

In my excitement at meeting a kindred spirit, I fear I dropped some unfortunate hints about the special denizen of the island that led Anna to become curious. Soon I discovered that she was prowling about the house late at night, searching for clues! (It was then, <u>most</u> providentially, that I first locked the door to the Tower Room.) Then she and her son took to exploring the island! I tried to protest but did not want to call too much attention to my distress—I felt that would only confirm her growing suspicions.

She spoke of capturing you-know-who and of immense riches and fame. I argued that magical creatures were only found in fairy tales and implied that I myself, though desperately wanting to believe, had been proven wrong time and time again and had become convinced that F and his kind are simply imaginary. Gradually, I believe, she came to agree with me. Her visit was <u>at last</u> drawing to a close, and I allowed myself a sigh of relief.

Then one morning Johann Pieter, who had risen at sunrise for a final walk along the beach, came <u>racing</u> into the house incoherent with excitement. He had discovered <u>tracks</u> on the beach, he said, <u>immense clawed footprints</u> that could only belong to a <u>you-know-what</u>—one who perhaps lived in a cave beneath the sea. His mother and I went with him to examine the miraculous tracks, but when we arrived, the water had washed them away. If, indeed, they were ever there—Johann Pieter was a <u>most</u> imaginative little boy and <u>very</u> eager to please his mother.

Anna, by then, however, had come to see her quest as a waste of time, but when she and Johann Pieter departed the island, I saved the photograph as a reminder to myself <u>never</u> to be so careless again! It was a narrow escape and one that I have <u>never</u> forgotten!

I wish I could be there to help, but I am <u>still</u> incapacitated with my broken ankle! The doctor tells me that it will be <u>at least</u> another four weeks before I can attempt to walk on it! (I have done

some experiments privately, and I suspect that he
is correct.) In any case, I trust that you will be able
to handle things on your own, in the best interests
of F.

> *With fondest regards,*
> *Aunt Mehitabel*

"What a nasty person," Sarah Emily said. "That Anna. Sneaking around like that. And lying."

"The worst is that she wanted to capture Fafnyr," Zachary said.

"I don't think the Awful Warning helps us much, though," Hannah said. "We didn't invite Mr. King here. He just came."

"Maybe he'll go away," Sarah Emily said hopefully. "Now that he's got Aunt Mehitabel's letter."

The children were sitting on the bed in Hannah's room. Buster, looking like a furry balloon with a smirk on its face, was comfortably asleep in Sarah Emily's lap. Zachary was tinkering with his tape recorder, which hadn't worked properly since Ben had jerked it out of his hands and dropped it on the sand. Something inside it seemed to be stuck. When Zachary pressed the PLAY button, it buzzed like a sick bumblebee or made sad little whirring sounds.

"Maybe he already left," said Hannah, looking brighter.

"Let's take a picnic to the north end of the island. We can see if the yacht is still there."

"I give up," Zachary said, tossing the tape recorder into a bureau drawer. "Let's go."

Mrs. Jones packed a picnic basket, stuffed with all their favorites: hard-boiled eggs, pickles, peanut-butter-and-banana sandwiches, and oatmeal cookies. Cheerfully, they set off across the island, Zachary in the lead, wearing his backpack, Hannah and Sarah Emily swinging the picnic basket between them. Hannah began to sing a song about how she loved to go a-wandering.

"I can't wait to get there and see that boat gone," said Zachary.

They turned right and cut through the fields, heading for the beach, just south of the place where Mr. King's company had made their camp. They climbed over a tumble of rounded rocks—Sarah Emily said they looked like baby hippopotamuses—and then scrambled to the top of a sandy dune, overgrown with scrub and grass, that sloped down to the beach. The tents were gone, but the great white yacht still rode at anchor off the shore.

"I knew it was too good to be true," Zachary said. He dropped down on the sand. "He never gives up, just like everybody says."

"Oh, come on, Zachary," said Hannah. "I think it's

going to be all right. He got Aunt Mehitabel's letter and he's packing up. They took down the tents, didn't they? I bet he'll be gone by this afternoon."

"I hope so," Sarah Emily said.

Zachary looked skeptical. "We might as well eat," he said.

As the children finished the last bites of their sandwiches, a figure appeared at the rail of the yacht's upper deck. It climbed down the metal ladder attached to the boat's side and dropped into a waiting motorboat. There was the sputter of a starting motor, and the boat turned in a wide smooth curve and headed toward the shore. As it grew closer, the children could see that the driver was Mr. J.P. King. When he was within hailing distance, he cut the motor and raised one hand, signaling to the children on the beach. "Permission to come ashore?" he shouted. He looked fit and friendly, like a kindly grandfather who took time to go to an exercise club.

The children exchanged worried looks.

"I suppose so," said Hannah.

Zachary stood up and lifted a hand in answer. "OK!" he shouted. "Temporarily!"

Mr. King landed the boat and sprang lightly out onto the sand. He was dressed as he had been at their previous meeting, in khaki slacks and a blue sweater, but now he wore a white cap with a black visor trimmed with gold braid. He walked briskly toward them across the beach and sat down on a rock next to the children's picnic site.

"A lovely place," he said.

"Did you get a letter from our aunt?" Hannah asked bluntly.

"I did indeed," said Mr. King, "and she made her position quite clear. Which is why, of course, I ordered my employees back to the yacht. I hate to think that there might be . . . unpleasant accusations later. However, in light of your aunt's uncooperative letter, I would like to discuss the present situation with you three. Let us put our cards on the table. You and I both know about the . . ."—he paused—"extraordinary beast . . . hidden on the island. Clearly your aunt is also aware of its existence. She, however, may not understand the implications of this animal's presence here. She is very elderly, is she not?"

"Aunt Mehitabel is old," Hannah said. "But she isn't *senile*. She understands everything. And if there *were* an extraordinary animal here, she would know what's best to do about it."

Mr. King nodded understandingly. "Of course," he said. "I'm sure her intentions are admirable. The very old, however, sometimes become—how shall I put it?—a bit hidebound, reluctant to move with the times. Or perhaps your aunt is simply unwilling to share her good fortune? That is what we're talking about, is it not? Sharing?"

"What do you mean?" Sarah Emily asked.

"The creature who lives on this island," Mr. King continued, "is a great natural treasure, perhaps the very last of its species alive on earth. Knowledge of its existence is a great wonder that all people on the planet have a right to share. Would it be right for one person to keep—let us say, the Grand Canyon—all to themselves? Besides, the care of this creature is too great a responsibility for one elderly woman and three children. It should be protected by the very best that modern science and technology have to offer."

He paused and glanced behind him, upward toward the rocky peak of Drake's Hill.

"What if this creature were to become ill, had you thought of that? Or if it were injured? Why, you children might not even be here to tend to it. By the time you finally arrived, it might be too late."

Hannah's eyes widened in concern, but she said nothing.

"I propose," Mr. King said, "to establish a special nature preserve, a vast territory devoted to this creature alone. There it would be utterly safe—and people would be able to see it and learn from it. Perhaps people could learn wonderful things. Surely you have studied about endangered species in school. Any scientist would tell you that this is the right thing to do."

He looked fixedly at each child in turn.

"This amazing animal deserves the best—the very best that money can buy. And I am willing to provide it. Don't say anything now. Just think about it. I'll get back to you in a day or two."

"Wait a minute," said Zachary as Mr. King rose to go. "All of this sounds generous and fair. But we don't like some of the things you've done. What about all those people on the island? Sneaking around all over the place? *Spying?*"

"That Ben was mean too," Sarah Emily put in. "He yanked Zachary's arm and broke his tape recorder."

"How unpleasant," Mr. King said. "I apologize. I was carried away by the excitement of my discovery. I will take care of the matter." He looked up toward the hill once more. "I am sure," he said, "that we can negotiate in an aboveboard, civilized manner for the best of all concerned."

He nodded to the children. "Good day," he said, and walked back across the sand to the motorboat. He climbed in, started the motor, and chugged rapidly away.

The children sat, silent, around the empty picnic basket.

Then Zachary said, "I never thought of that before. Maybe we *are* being selfish. Think of all the special efforts being made to take care of endangered animals.

Like the California condor and the Siberian tiger and the spotted owl. Doesn't Fafnyr deserve the support of the whole world? Wouldn't he be safer?"

"He *is* safe," Sarah Emily said. "He's protected, right here. Aunt Mehitabel trusted us to protect him and keep him and his cave a secret."

"But what if Fafnyr got sick?" Hannah said. "We wouldn't know what to do. Mr. King is right. We might not even be here. Fafnyr could *die* and we wouldn't know."

"I don't know what's the right thing to do," Zachary said miserably. "What if Aunt Mehitabel is wrong?"

"We don't have to do anything for a day or two," Hannah said. "Not until Mr. King comes back."

"Let's go see Fafnyr," Sarah Emily said.

"It's too late today," said Zachary. "We'll have to come back tomorrow."

"She," said Hannah firmly. They were standing on the wide ledge above the ocean at the entrance to the dragon's cave. "Don't get mixed up because she doesn't like it. It's *she*. Remember?"

The third dragon head, as the children had learned last summer, was female.

The three children stepped through the dark entrance of the cave, and Zachary switched on his flashlight. They trudged steadily downward, breathing in the spicy odor of dragon: wood smoke, cinnamon, a tangy whiff of incense. Soon the flashlight picked up the scintillating flash of golden dragon scales. There was the sound of a heavy body shifting on the cave floor and a hissing noise, like the sound of a gas stove turning on. The dragon flamed and the cave filled with soft light. The third dragon head was awake. Its eyes were a cool luminous silver. It lowered its head toward the children, bending down first to Sarah Emily, then to Zachary, and finally Hannah.

"We are delighted at your return," the dragon said ceremoniously. It surveyed each of the children assessingly, then gave an approving nod.

"Field hockey?" it said. "Rockets? Piano lessons? Excellent. It is always rewarding to see the young improving their minds."

Then, suddenly, it bent even lower, bringing the silver eyes level with the children's faces. Its voice became filled with concern.

"Something is wrong," it said.

"Oh, Fafnyr," Sarah Emily said, her voice breaking. "Everything is so awful."

"The insufferably persistent person in the boat?" the dragon said. It wrinkled its nose in distaste.

"He knows all about you," Zachary said. "He seems to know everything. And he has this plan . . ."

"Tell me about it," the dragon said.

The children explained.

"He says that you could be the very last of your kind."

"An endangered species."

"All the world deserves to know about you, he says. It's selfish of us to keep you a secret all for ourselves."

"And what if you were sick or hurt? We wouldn't know how to help you."

"So he wants," Zachary summed up, "to build a special nature preserve, just for you. A place where you'd be taken care of. And you'd be safe forever."

The dragon listened patiently, unmoving, except for the slow blinking of its silver eyes.

"I see," it said when they had finished.

A silence fell.

Then Sarah Emily ran forward and threw her arms around the dragon's leg, pressing her face against the golden scales.

"We don't know what to do, Fafnyr," she said. Her eyes were filled with tears. "We don't know what's right and what's wrong. Everything is muddly."

The dragon lifted a golden claw and gently smoothed Sarah Emily's hair.

"I think," it said, "that I should tell you a story."

"But, Fafnyr . . ." Zachary began.

The dragon stopped him with a lifted golden claw.

"We'll get to all that," it said. "First, listen."

The children sank down on the warm cave floor. Zachary sat cross-legged. Hannah and Sarah Emily leaned back against the dragon's golden tail. As the dragon spoke, the cave walls seemed to shimmer and dissolve. The children felt a breath of warm wind on their cheeks. There was a sound of soft laughter, a sweet smell of honeysuckle and gardenia flowers. The children again found themselves in another place and time, seeing the world through someone else's eyes.

The Silver-Eyed Dragon's Story
SALLIE

"Sallie," the dragon began, "was born a slave. Her great-great-grandfather had been brought to North America from Africa in chains in a slave ship. Sallie was dark brown, the color of milk chocolate, with bright brown eyes and curly black hair in pigtails, tied up with scraps of calico. She lived with her mother and father and her little brother, Jamie, in a tiny cabin in back of the Big House on a cotton plantation in Alabama in the days before the Civil War. Sallie's mother worked in the kitchen of the Big House, and Sallie's father was a blacksmith. He could make anything out of iron: horseshoes, hinges, shovels, nails, even garden gates. . . ."

There were children in the Big House, too. The daughter of the family, Harriet, was just Sallie's age. Harriet's life was very different from Sallie's. Harriet wore muslin dresses with long silk sashes, embroidered pantalettes, and satin dancing slippers. She had a governess named Miss Witherspoon. Harriet studied geography, arithmetic, and French, and she was learning how to play the harp. Harriet complained all the time about her lessons. It didn't seem fair, Sallie thought. Sallie would have given anything to go to school. She wanted to learn how to read.

Harriet couldn't understand why Sallie was unhappy. After all, everybody knew that this was just the way things were. Sallie had plenty to eat and a place to live. Harriet's father was a good master. The slaves even had special parties every year at Christmastime. But Harriet, Sallie thought, simply didn't know what it was really like to be a slave. Nothing, Sallie knew, could make up for the biggest difference between them. Harriet was free. No one could ever sell her away from her mother and father.

Today the sun was hot in the dooryard of the little cabin, but Sallie was so cold that she had goose bumps on her arms. She was afraid. A rumor was flying through the slave quarters. The news came from Martha Jane, Harriet's mother's personal maid. Martha Jane always knew everything that went on in the Big House. Harriet's father had gambling debts, Martha Jane said. He owed thousands of dollars and he had no way to pay. Some of the slaves would have to be sold. "Who?" people already were asking each other secretly. "Who will it be?" Sallie knew that her father, a trained blacksmith, was a very valuable slave. And Sallie's mother was in tears. There had been long whispered conversations at night in the dark after Sallie and Jamie were thought to be sound asleep. Sallie had kept quite still beneath her patch-work quilt, trying to breathe evenly, listening with all her might. Her father spoke of the free territory in the North, of secret paths and hiding places, of the Underground Railroad. Her mother spoke of fugitives, of whippings, of slave catchers, and bloodhounds. Sallie knew that her parents were planning to run away. And she knew that they were afraid.

"Sallie!" A call came from the terrace of the Big House. "Sallie!" It was old Eliza, who had taken care of Harriet's mother when she was a little girl, then of Harriet and her brothers when they were babies. "The young mistress wants you!" Harriet, Sallie thought, probably wanted her to braid her hair—or to help her dress her dolls or to mend a torn gown.

Not now, Sallie thought. I can't stand to go to the Big House now. Let Harriet think that Eliza couldn't find me.

She jumped to her feet and whisked around the corner of the cabin. Unnoticed, she edged along the log walls, then scampered across the garden, grown tall with beans and corn, and into the woods on the far side. As soon as she was hidden by the trees, she ran until she could run no more. Then she sat down on a fallen tree trunk and cried. She felt angry and helpless and frightened. What if they ran? They would be leaving their home, their friends. The plantation was all that Sallie had ever known. But what if they stayed? They would sell her father. Maybe even her mother. She and Jamie would be left alone. Or maybe they would sell Jamie too. He was a strong, healthy little boy, even if he was only six years old. Sallie wiped her face on her apron. She felt as though she hated the whole world.

When she looked up, she realized that she was lost. Nothing looked familiar and there were no paths in sight. She got to her feet and began to walk, wandering, not knowing what to do or where to go. The forest grew denser. The trees were bigger and closer together. The underbrush was thicker. Thorns pricked her bare feet and tore at her apron and her red calico dress. Finally Sallie came upon a tumbled pile of rocks. A hill, she thought. If I climb to the top, I'll be able to see a long way. Then perhaps I can figure out where I am. She started to scramble up the sun-warmed stones.

Halfway to the top she stopped and stared, her eyes wide with fright. There was a gaping hole in the rocks—a cave—and sunning itself in the cave door was a creature like nothing Sallie had ever seen before.

It was huge and it was pure gold. It was covered with glittering scales. It had a long arrow-pointed tail, a pair of smooth webbed wings, and—Sallie gasped—three heads on long golden necks. Two of the heads were coiled low on the creature's shoulders, the third stretched out straight in front of its body. As Sallie watched, the third head opened its eyes. They were a pure gleaming silver, the color of the tea set in the Big House parlor. Sallie had to polish that tea set sometimes, when Harriet's mother was expecting company. The silver eyes were looking, Sallie realized, straight at her.

For a moment, she was deathly afraid. Then her heart stopped racing and she grew calm. It doesn't matter, Sallie told herself. Everything is so dreadful. I might as well be eaten by a monster. Things could hardly be worse.

She must have spoken out loud, because the creature replied.

"I do not," the creature said in outraged tones, "eat children. Especially not sniveling little girls."

Sallie felt her temper rise. "I am *not* sniveling," she snapped.

"Sniveling," the creature said. "Most definitely." It had lifted its golden head. It glared at Sallie, and Sallie glared right back.

Then Sallie's temper evaporated, overcome by curiosity.

"What are you?" she asked. "I've never seen anything like you before."

The creature flexed ten polished golden claws. "I," it said, "am a dragon. A tridrake, to be precise. *Tri* means *three*, in Latin. It refers to the three heads. The sleeping heads belong to my brothers. I, of course, am female. And you?"

"My name is Sallie," Sallie said. "I live on the plantation. . . ." She tried to gesture. Then she dropped her hand. "I'm not sure where it is anymore," she confessed. "I think I'm lost."

"And how did you come to be wandering through this—previously quite private—part of the forest?" the dragon asked.

Sallie suddenly started to cry again. She put her face down on her knees and sobbed. Then she heard a voice above her head. It was the dragon.

"My dear child," the dragon said. "My dear young lady, please don't cry. Whatever I said—please accept my apologies. Is there anything I can do?" A golden claw reached out and gently stroked Sallie's hair.

Sallie shook her head. "There's nothing anybody can do," she said. And then, because the dragon had a kindly listening look, she told it all that was happening. She told about Harriet and the Big House, about Harriet's father and his gambling debts, about the slaves being sold, about wanting to learn to read, about wanting to be free. About her parents' secret plan to run away. About the slave catchers and the whippings. About how frightened she was. The words tumbled over each other as Sallie talked. She felt as though no one had ever listened to her so carefully before.

When she had finished, the dragon heaved a great sigh and turned its head away from her, staring off into the forest.

"An unspeakable practice, slavery," the dragon said. "Barbaric. Abominable. A hideous custom. But," it continued bolsteringly, "all will eventually come right, my dear. Humans can be dense, but they do eventually learn. I predict that in less than a century all"— the dragon twisted its mouth as though the word had a bad taste—"*slavery* here will be a thing of the past."

"A century?" asked Sallie.

"A hundred years," the dragon said. "Again, from the Latin. A useful language, Latin. Century," it repeated. "Centennial. Centimeter. Centipede."

"*A hundred years?*" Sallie said, horrified. "Nothing will get better for *a hundred years?*" Her eyes filled with tears again.

"It could, of course, be sooner," the dragon said helpfully. "Depending on the political and economic climate."

Sallie mopped her face on her apron. "But we can't wait," she said. "I — my family—we need help right now."

The dragon, looking annoyed with itself, shook its head. "How foolish of me," it said. "I forget how short-lived you creatures are. Of course you need a speedier solution. Your parents are quite right. Of course you must run away." It closed its eyes and seemed lost for a moment in thought.

"Any new endeavor is difficult, my dear," it said finally. "It is always hard to leave the old and familiar for the new and unknown. It takes great courage. But you will find that the rewards are well worth the struggle. Think of caterpillars."

"*Caterpillars?*" repeated Sallie, startled.

"They don't *stay* caterpillars," the dragon said. "They spin cocoons and turn into butterflies. It can't be easy for them, poor things, leaving their safe little lives on the ground, where they were used to crawling around on things and munching leaves. But then

113

they fly on glorious wings. And so will you, my dear. You'll see."

Then it said, "Please hold out your hand."

Doubtfully Sallie held out her hand. The dragon lifted a forefoot, leaned forward, and swiftly pricked Sallie's hand with one golden claw. Sallie felt a sharp pang, which quickly turned into a soothing warmth. In the middle of her palm, the dragon's claw had left a gleaming fleck of gold.

"It is the mark of a Dragon Friend," the dragon said softly. "All dragons will know you by it and will help you in times of need."

Awed, Sallie touched a finger to the golden mark.

"Thank you," she whispered.

The dragon pointed through the trees. "Go that way," it said. "Your home—or perhaps I should say your profligate owner's home—lies in that direction."

Sallie got slowly to her feet.

"Good luck, my dear," the dragon said. "Be brave. Remember the butterfly."

THE ESCAPE

When Sallie arrived home, her family was in the cabin, gathered around the rough wooden table, too upset to eat their evening meal.

"Where have you been, Sallie?" her mother asked as Sallie opened the door. "They've been looking for you all afternoon up at the Big House. Miss Harriet is mighty angry, Eliza says."

Sallie sat down on the bench next to Jamie and reached for a piece of corn bread. She took a big bite.

"I don't care," she said. "I'm not going to do what Harriet says anymore."

Her mother frowned. "Sallie," she began gently.

Sallie got up from the bench and walked to the

door. She opened it and peered out, to make sure no one was listening. There was nobody nearby. She came back to the table and sat down again.

"Mama," she said. "Daddy. Please. Are we going to run away?"

Sallie's parents exchanged a long look. Sallie's father put an arm around Sallie's mother and hugged her close.

"Yes," Sallie's father said. "It's the only way."

He grinned ruefully. "I'm a very valuable property, you know. I'd go a long way toward paying for the master's poker games."

Sallie's mother put a hand on his arm.

"We'll go tomorrow night," she said. "As soon as it's dark. We were waiting until the last minute to tell you. I know it's going to be hard on you children, and it's dangerous—but it will be far worse if we stay here."

Sallie's father turned to the children. "And you cannot say anything about this to anyone," he said. "Not one word, even to your best friends. Not to Amanda, Sallie, or to Samuel, Jamie. Especially not to Martha Jane. No one must know."

"There will be trouble enough when they find we're gone," Sallie's mother said. "It will be safer for all our friends, the less they know."

Sallie spent the next day working at the Big House. Harriet was cross with her.

"Where were you yesterday?" she said. "I wanted you. You're supposed to do what *I* say. I could have you whipped, you know, if you don't do what you're told."

"Yes, Miss Harriet," Sallie said meekly. She fanned Harriet while she practiced the harp. She made Harriet's bed and dusted her bedroom and mended her pink dress, which had a torn hem. And all the while she counted the hours until night would fall.

I'll never work in this house again, she thought to herself, hugging her secret close. I'll never see *you* again, she thought, helping Harriet dress to go downstairs for supper. On the way home, she slammed the back door of the Big House behind her. Never again, Sallie said to herself. She repeated it to herself over and over again, like a little song. Never again. Never again.

Back in the little cabin, Sallie and her family collected a very few things to take on their long journey. A bundle of tools for her father—"They owe me that much," her father said grimly—a few scraps of clothing, some pennies Sallie's mother had earned selling eggs, a package of cold corn bread, and a bracelet of carved wooden beads.

"That belonged to your great-great-grandfather," Sallie's father said. "It came all the way from Africa."

Soon it was dark and the slave quarters were silent. Nothing stirred.

"You can't make a single sound," Sallie's father whispered. "Even if you stub your toe, Jamie, and it really hurts—you must stay absolutely quiet. If you make a noise, they might find us and bring us back, and that would be terrible. We would be beaten, whipped. We would all be sold. We would never see each other again."

Jamie's eyes were wide and frightened. "I'll be very quiet," he whispered.

Sallie nodded.

Silently they slipped out the cabin door, around the side of the house, through the garden, and into the woods, the way Sallie had gone the day before. Sallie's father pointed up at the sky.

"That's the way we're going," he said. "North. See the Drinking Gourd?"

"Where?" Jamie whispered.

"Those seven stars," his father explained. "See how they're shaped like a dipper? See the long handle and the cup? As long as we keep those stars in front of us, we'll know we're going in the right direction."

"*Hurry*," Sallie's mother said. "We want to get as far as we can before daybreak."

They walked for many nights. Often they walked through streams, and once they crossed a muddy swamp, in water up to their waists. Sallie hated that swamp. The sticky bottom felt awful.

"It's the best thing we could have found," her father said. "Sometimes slave catchers chase after escaping slaves with dogs. The dogs are trained to follow a person's scent. But they can't follow a scent through water."

They were hungry all the time.

Sometimes they found nuts and berries in the woods. Sometimes Sallie's father caught fish, but not often, because it was very dangerous to light a cooking fire.

They slept in thickets and in caves, and once in a deserted barn in a little clearing, its roof half fallen in.

"We must be almost there," Sallie's father said one day, when Jamie complained that his feet were tired. "It can't be much farther now. We'll come to a big river. It's called the Ohio. And on the other side, it's all free country. Once we get there, we'll be free."

But the very next night disaster struck. They were walking along a little grass track through the woods, single file, their way lit only by the moon. There was no sound but the rustle of wind in the leaves. Then, behind them in the distance, there came the sound of barking dogs.

Sallie's mother looked back in alarm.

"Amos!" she whispered. "What's that?"

"Let's go faster," said Sallie's father. "There's nowhere to hide here."

They hurried along the little path, as fast as they could go, tripping and stumbling. Sallie's heart began to pound with fear.

We're so close, she thought, so close. They *can't* catch us now.

Behind them the barking of dogs got louder, and there was a sound of horses' hooves and the jingling of harnesses.

"Those dogs smell something, boys!" a man's deep voice shouted. "Runaways!"

The trees suddenly gave way to a long grassy field. Far across it, Sallie could see the dark gleam of flowing water. It was the river.

"Might as well give it up," the deep voice shouted. "We've got you now!"

A dog howled.

Sallie's mother stumbled and fell. When she tried to get to her feet again, her face twisted with pain. "It's my ankle!" she gasped. "Amos . . ."

Sallie's father handed his bundle of tools to Sallie, and bent and scooped Sallie's mother up in his arms.

"We'll never make it," Sallie's mother said.

"Run!" Sallie's father shouted. "Sallie! Jamie! *Run!*"

Oh please, Sallie thought to herself. Oh please, let us make it across the river. Oh please . . .

And then, miraculously, above them in the sky, where a moment ago there had been nothing but moon and stars, appeared a great flash of glittering gold.

"Dear Lord," said Sallie's father.

It was the dragon. It hovered high above the trees, long golden neck arched, golden wings outspread.

Sallie's mother hid her face in her father's shirt front.

Jamie burst into tears.

Sallie stepped quickly forward. "It's all right," she said. "It's a dragon. And a friend. I met her in the woods before we ran away. I should have told you. But I know she won't hurt us. I think she's here to help us."

"We could use it," Sallie's father said. Behind them the baying of the dogs was growing louder.

The dragon reared back in the air. There was a whooshing sound of indrawn breath and a sudden roar of flame. The night exploded with light. The dragon shone sun-golden in the air, blowing a blaze of blue flame. At the edge of the wood, the thicket began to burn. Fire licked across the grass. Bushes crackled and burst into flame. Light flickered across the faces of Sallie's parents and brother. Jamie had stopped crying.

There was now a wall of fire between Sallie's family and their pursuers. They heard, faintly, the sound of startled yells and of dogs retreating, yelping now in terror.

A hot wind struck them. The dragon landed before them in the grass. Politely it inclined its golden head.

Sallie's father stepped forward.

"We have no words to thank you, sir," he began.

"Ma'am," Sallie hissed hastily behind him.

"Ma'am," Sallie's father said. "You have saved our lives." He paused. "More than our lives. You have given us our freedom."

The dragon impatiently shook its head. "You have *taken back* your freedom," it said. "It was yours all along."

It gestured toward the river with a golden claw.

"There on the bank," the dragon said, "near that little clump of trees, you'll find a rowboat. It was left there by the farmer who lives in the house across the river. You can just see the light in his window from here. He leaves the boat there for runaways like yourselves. He is a conductor on the Underground Railroad. He will help you."

Slowly Sallie and her family began to walk across the field toward the river, with the golden dragon pacing by their side. The wind in their faces now was cool and fresh, blowing toward them off the river. It smelled sweetly green.

Sallie's father took deep breaths.

"Smell that," he said. "The air of freedom."

Sallie's mother suddenly gave a little laugh. "I just realized," she said, "we don't even have a name. Our old master—we certainly don't want his anymore."

"No name?" Sallie said. "You mean we can just pick one of our own?"

The dragon had paused in the grass. It held its golden head very high, staring off across the dark river.

"In the matter of a name," the dragon said solemnly, "I would be most honored if you would take mine."

The Discovery in the Dictionary

The children shifted on the cave floor. The dragon had fallen silent.

"Did they really take your name?" Sarah Emily asked. "Goldenwings? That must have sounded a little strange."

The dragon bent down toward her with an incredulous look on its face. *"Strange?"* it repeated, in an offended tone. *"Strange?* You find my name *strange*?"

Sarah Emily hastily backtracked. "Not at all," she said. "It's a beautiful name. I didn't mean anything bad. It's just a little unusual, that's all."

The dragon regarded her suspiciously for a moment. It gave a small snort.

"Go on," Sarah Emily said. "What happened to Sallie? Did they get across the river? Were they all right?"

"They crossed the river," the dragon said. "They settled down in Ohio, in free country. Sallie's father opened a little blacksmith shop. They were safe, but Sallie worried about all the people they had left behind. When she grew up, she decided to do something about it. She went back down south, following secret paths through the woods, and helped many runaways find their way north, out of slavery, into freedom. Then the Civil War came and Abraham Lincoln took care of all the rest. And Sallie learned to read. After the war, she became a schoolteacher."

"She flew," Hannah said softly.

"What happened to Jamie?" Zachary asked.

The dragon's face grew sad. "He joined the Union army during the war," it said. "He was killed at Gettysburg. Fighting for freedom."

Zachary, still sitting cross-legged at the dragon's feet, said quietly, "What's worth fighting for . . ."

"I know why you told us Sallie's story just now," Hannah said. "And those other stories too. This is all about freedom, isn't it? We've been so confused, Fafnyr. Mr. King was almost making sense, but now that I think about it, I see that he was all wrong."

"I don't think Mr. King really wants to protect Fafnyr," Zachary said. "I think he just wants another valuable possession."

"Fafnyr isn't property," Sarah Emily chimed in. "It isn't up to us to share him. He doesn't belong to us. He doesn't belong to anybody except to himself."

125

"Herself," Hannah whispered quickly.

The golden dragon nodded.

"I thought you'd work it out," it said, sounding pleased.

Then it gave an indignant snort.

"As if any dragon would fall for that," it said scornfully. "*Nature preserve,* indeed."

"We don't want to accept Mr. King's proposal," Zachary said, "but we're just kids—and he's rich and powerful and grown up. What if he won't take no for an answer? What can we *do*?"

The dragon waved a golden claw. "In life," it said impressively, "one often reaches decision points."

"I don't understand," Hannah said.

The dragon gave a tiny snort. "Take, for example," it said, "the moment before breakfast."

"Before *breakfast*?" Zachary repeated blankly.

"Precisely," the dragon said. "A prototypic decision point. You could choose to have oatmeal, you see, or mutton chops, bran flakes or jellybeans, toast or tacos. It's quite simple. You survey the alternatives and pick the best one. Even the youngest dragon can do it."

"But . . ." Sarah Emily began.

"Jellybeans would be a poor choice," the dragon said severely. "They are nutritionally limited. And, of course, so small."

"But I don't see . . ." Sarah Emily began again.

"Of course you don't," the dragon said. "You're not using your head."

It gave an enormous yawn.

"When confronted with a problem, one studies the alternatives, selects the best solution, and proceeds with it. It's very simple." It looked at the children down the length of its golden nose. "You must learn, my dears, to reason like a dragon."

Supper was over. Hannah, Zachary, and Sarah Emily were in Aunt Mehitabel's front parlor, where Hannah was teaching Sarah Emily to play chess. Zachary, who had eaten three bowls of chocolate pudding and was feeling lazy, lay on his stomach in front of the glass-fronted bookcase, idly reading the titles of books.

"The ones with the little pointy hats are bishops," Hannah said. "They move diagonally, like this. Come on, S.E., pay attention."

"I can't help it," Sarah Emily said. "All the pieces are so pretty. Look at the castles with their little turrets. And my queen has a crown with teeny silver beads."

"She's lined up with my bishop," Hannah said patiently. "The bishops move diagonally."

"*Oh!*" Sarah Emily said. She hastily swooped her queen out of the way. "I see."

"Nobody could read these books," said Zachary from his place on the floor. "They're awful. Listen: *The Collected Spiritual Ramblings of Dr. Theophilus Bumbrage. A Botanical Description of the Duckweeds of Delaware. A Discourse on the Jungle Fowl of India and Ceylon.*"

"Where's Ceylon?" Sarah Emily asked. "What are jungle fowl?"

"Ceylon is called Sri Lanka now," Hannah said, moving a carved green pawn. "It's an island in the Indian Ocean. And jungle fowl are sort of like chickens. Wild chickens. You can't move that castle there, S.E. They only go in straight lines."

"And then there are all these weird dictionaries," Zachary said, wiggling forward on his elbows. "There's one in Sanskrit and one in Cherokee."

He opened a glass panel and pulled out a book.

"This one is German. But the letters are all funny, like those big old-fashioned Bibles."

"Check," Hannah said.

"Donnerschlag," Zachary read in a threatening voice. "That means thunderclap. *Lebkuchen.* That's gingerbread. *Schweigepflicht.* That's what we have. It's a pledge of secrecy."

"Schweigepflicht," Sarah Emily said, and giggled.

"Check," Hannah said again.

Sarah Emily stared dismally at the board. "I don't think I'm any good at chess," she said.

128

"Sure you are," Hannah said. "It's a hard game, that's all. You have to keep thinking ahead all the time. Consider the alternatives like Faf . . . F says. You have to move your king, see?"

"King," Zachary said, busily flipping dictionary pages.

Then suddenly he made a startled exclamation and sat straight up. He looked shocked. His face had gone so pale that the freckles stood out.

Hannah leaped up from the chessboard.

"What's wrong?" she said. "Zachary, are you sick?"

"It's *König*," Zachary said in a shaken voice, pointing to the dictionary page.

"*König?*" Sarah Emily looked confused.

"*König*," Zachary repeated. "It means *king* in German." Now he was talking so fast that his words tumbled over each other. "Don't you remember Aunt Mehitabel's letter? The boy was named Johann Pieter König. But he would be all grown up now. Getting old, even."

He looked from Hannah to Sarah Emily and back again.

"King. König. Don't you see? I think Johann Pieter has come back. I think he's J.P. King."

Caught

"J.P. King is Johann Pieter?" Sarah Emily said.

"It makes sense," Hannah said slowly. "He saw the track on the beach, remember? He must have known it was real, no matter what anybody else said. He must have been thinking about it all these years. And now he's come back."

"He never gives up," Zachary said. "Everybody says so."

"We have to warn Fafnyr," Sarah Emily said in a trembling voice.

"Nothing's going to happen tonight," Hannah said reassuringly. "They don't know where the cave is yet, S.E."

"We'll go first thing in the morning and warn him," Zachary said. "Maybe Fafnyr will have to go away for a while."

"Find another Resting Place?" Sarah Emily said. Her eyes filled with tears.

"Nobody wants that, S.E.," Hannah said miserably. "But what if it's the only way to keep him safe?"

Tears rolled down Sarah Emily's cheeks.

The next morning looked just like the children felt. It was cold, dismal, and gray. The sky was dark and threatening, heavy with clouds, and the wind had a sharp edge to it. Walking into it felt like being slapped with wet sheets. They plodded single-file along the familiar path, sweatshirt hoods pulled up to protect their ears. Instead of sneakers, they wore hiking boots, and over their sweatshirts they wore zippered vests. Everybody felt too miserable to talk. Sarah Emily had barely been able to choke down her breakfast, and even Zachary had been unable to finish his fourth piece of buttered toast.

"Trouble ahead," Hannah suddenly said.

Two figures, standing side by side, waited silently for them at the foot of Drake's Hill. The first was J.P. King. He was dressed in a leather aviator's jacket and a canvas hat with a cord that fastened under his chin. A leather bag with a strap hung from one shoulder. Beside him stood Mr. Chang, now in loose black trousers and a black quilted jacket. He was still wearing his elaborately embroidered cap.

"Greetings," called Mr. King, with an affable smile. Then, as the children drew closer: "I understand that you have already met my compatriot, Mr. Chang."

Mr. Chang gave them the slightest of bows.

"He is an esteemed scholar at the Archaeological Institute of Beijing," Mr. King continued, "and an expert in the history and lore of magical creatures. He is famed in academic circles for his monographs on imperial dragons in the art and literature of the Tang dynasty."

Sarah Emily gave a little gasp.

"I see you understand the connection," Mr. King said pleasantly.

"We know who you are," Zachary said. "You're Johann Pieter König. You've been here before."

Mr. King nodded delightedly.

"Clever," he said. "Very clever, young man. Though I suspect your aunt may have given you a clue or two. A quick-witted lady, your aunt, though a bit too trusting. You can't be too cautious when you have a secret, you know."

"She thought you and your mother were her friends," Hannah said coldly.

"She told us what happened," Zachary said at the same time.

"Ah," Mr. King said, nodding several times quickly. "Then you understand why I am here. I *know*, you see, that this island conceals a dragon."

"Why would you think that?" Hannah said, making her eyes wide and innocent.

Mr. King was not taken in.

"Because I saw it," he snapped. "Flying at sunrise. A great golden beast with a blaze of sun behind it and a golden glitter on the water . . ."

"It sounds to me like a mirage," Zachary said.

There was a tense pause.

"You three are very young," Mr. King said in his earlier, more pleasant tone. "You have no conception of the implications. My research and that of Mr. Chang here"—he made a gesture toward the silent black-clad figure at his side—"indicate that there are indeed still such creatures left alive, miraculous beings from the ancient dawn of time, hidden in secluded spots about the globe, rarely showing themselves to humans. This is a fabulous discovery, with incalculable possibilities for wealth, fame . . ."

He bent down, resting his hands on his knees, and spoke directly to Sarah Emily. "Have you never had a beloved pet, my dear? A cat, perhaps, or a dog? And wasn't it better cared for in your home than it would have been left to fend for itself in the wild? What could be wrong with taking this poor dumb animal out of its present uncomfortable habitat to a place of near-infinite luxury?"

"Fafnyr's not poor and dumb!" Zachary shouted. "He can talk! And he's good and wise!"

"Well, well," Mr. King said, straightening up. "Since you know that this—did you call him Fafnyr?—can speak, then you most certainly must know where this Fafnyr *lives*."

He made a quick gesture toward Mr. Chang. Together the two men lunged forward. J.P. King seized Zachary and Mr. Chang seized the two girls.

"There's really no need for all this fuss," Mr. King said testily, gripping Zachary's arms. "Many animals speak, which deceives us into thinking they possess more intelligence than they actually do. Parrots, for example. Myna birds."

"It's not the same!" Hannah shouted.

"No, no," said Mr. King, as Zachary started to squirm and struggle. "I really wouldn't do that, young man. No harm will come to you or your lovely sisters provided you all do just exactly as I say. Once you have led me to this beast's lair, you children will be free to go. For the moment, however, I fear you must consider yourselves to be my . . . guests."

Zachary threw his sisters a despairing look.

"This won't do you any good," Hannah said angrily. "You'll never get near him. He's very large and fierce. And he can breathe fire."

"He could turn you into a human torch," Zachary said spitefully.

"Oh, there's no need to worry about me," said Mr. King, no longer sounding pleasant at all. He patted the leather bag at his side. "I have not come unprepared. I have in here a specially made dart gun, loaded with a penetrating capsule that contains a powerful sedative—

enough to render an entire herd of African elephants safely unconscious. I am sure it will have a similar effect on your friend."

"You can't shoot Fafnyr with some horrible drug!" Sarah Emily cried.

Mr. King looked annoyed. "Oh, come, come," he said testily. "I don't plan to *hurt* the creature. The sedative will simply immobilize it until I can arrange proper transport."

He nodded to Mr. Chang.

"The boy and I will lead the way," he said briskly.

Then he turned to Zachary.

"Move along, young man," he said sharply. "I haven't got all day. Up this way, is it? Well, climb, young man, climb!"

✌ 18 ✌

Dragon Friends

They climbed.

Zachary and Mr. King were in the lead. Mr. Chang and the girls followed. But soon the two groups grew apart, as Zachary, prodded by Mr. King, moved on at an increasingly faster pace. Mr. Chang, on the other hand, was a reluctant walker. Once he paused to look for a stone in his shoe; then again he stopped to catch his breath. Gradually he, Hannah, and Sarah Emily fell farther and farther behind. Zachary and Mr. King had reached the massive heap of step-like gray rocks that formed the top of Drake's Hill and had begun to scramble up.

"We'd better hurry," Hannah said unhappily. "They're getting way ahead of us."

"That is best for the moment," Mr. Chang said.

"Best for what?" Sarah Emily said, with a miserable catch in her voice.

"We need to talk for a bit, you and I," Mr. Chang said softly.

He opened his hand and extended it toward the children, palm upward. There, in the very middle of his thin ivory-colored hand, gleamed a glittering fleck of gold.

"No, I do not know your Fafnyr," Mr. Chang said. "I knew the dragon Angwyn."

His eyes grew soft as if he were looking at something much loved and far away.

"Long ago when I was a boy in China, I saved her egg when an earthquake threw it from its Resting Place. I have been most honored."

"But I don't understand," Sarah Emily said. "You're a Dragon Friend. Why are you working with Mr. King?"

"He had heard of my studies, and he traveled to meet me in Beijing," Mr. Chang said. "He hinted of a marvelous discovery. A dragon—a Great One—living hidden on an island in America. We arrived here and our search began. The members of the crew were kept in the dark. They were never told what they were looking for. Rare geological deposits were suggested, and there was some mention of passenger pigeons. I alone knew the nature of Mr. King's quest, but only recently did I discover what his true intentions were. But by then I could do nothing but watch and prepare to interfere when the proper time came."

"I think the proper time has come," Hannah said, sounding stronger.

"If only we're not too late," Sarah Emily said urgently.

"Trust the dragon," Mr. Chang said.

By now they had reached the great rock steps. Zachary and Mr. King were high above them, nearing the shelf that edged around the hillside to the broad platform overlooking the sea.

"*Hurry,*" Sarah Emily said fiercely. "They're almost there."

They scrambled frantically from rock to rock, the girls in front, Mr. Chang gamely following behind.

"Someone's yelling," Hannah said suddenly.

"It's Zachary!" said Sarah Emily.

They dashed around the last turn of the ledge and stumbled out onto the broad stone platform. Mr. King and Zachary stood at the entrance to the cave. Both looked red-faced and furious.

"Don't be ridiculous!" Mr. King was saying angrily. "And keep your voice down! You might alarm the creature! Don't you understand? That animal is priceless! Priceless! You young fools have no idea what you have here!"

Mr. Chang had a hand pressed to his chest and was panting for breath.

"Keep them quiet while we enter the cave, Chang," Mr. King snapped.

Then, abruptly, he seemed to change his mind.

"No, come along, all of you," he ordered. "You children can lead the way. If the beast is as fond of you as you appear to be of it, you should make quite effective human shields. Breathing fire in an enclosed space is quite lethal, you know. I feel certain that your reptilian friend will be too wise to risk your lives."

He pushed Zachary toward the entrance of the cave and gestured impatiently at Hannah and Sarah Emily to follow.

"Follow me, Chang," Mr. King said.

Reluctantly, huddled close together, the three children entered the dragon's cave. Usually as they stepped into the cinnamon-scented darkness, they were filled with a Christmas-morning sense of delighted anticipation. Today they felt nothing but despair. There was the scratchy sound of a zipper as Zachary opened his backpack and groped for his flashlight. He pulled it out and switched it on. At the same time, behind them, Mr. King flicked on a larger and more powerful beam. They moved slowly downward, descending into the depths of the cave.

"He's a Dragon Friend," Hannah muttered hastily to Zachary. "Mr. Chang is. He's on our side."

"But what will we *do*?" Sarah Emily whispered desperately.

"Maybe Fafnyr will think of something," Hannah whispered back. "Mr. Chang said to trust the dragon."

"Fafnyr can't think of something if he's taken by surprise," Zachary whispered. "We have to warn him."

"But *how*?" Hannah whispered. "He'll be asleep."

"Quiet!" Mr. King ordered sharply from behind them.

"Let's run ahead," Sarah Emily whispered. "And yell as loud as we can. It's the best we can do. At least it will give Fafnyr a chance."

"*Quiet!*" Mr. King hissed.

"All right," Zachary whispered. "Let's do it. On the count of three."

"We're almost there," Hannah whispered. "Ready? One. Two. *Three!*"

The children sprang forward, darting away from Mr. King, feet thumping on the uneven stone floor, shouting at the top of their lungs.

"*Fafnyr! Danger!*"

"*Fafnyr! Wake up!*"

"*Fafnyr! Look out!!*"

Behind them they could hear Mr. Chang running and roaring a warning too.

There was a sound of rapid movement in the darkness, a thunderous clatter, a sharp hiss, and a brilliant flash of gold. The cave burst into light. The dragon

140

stood toweringly erect in the center of the cave, its golden wings outspread. All three heads were awake. The three pairs of eyes, brilliant green, blue, and silver, glared at J.P. King.

Mr. King took a step backward, fumbling in his leather shoulder bag. He gave the dragon a measuring look, his glance sweeping from the three towering heads to the flared golden wings to the tip of the gleaming arrow-pointed tail.

"Impressive," Mr. King said. "And much larger than I had imagined." A gloating note crept into his voice. "Very impressive indeed."

"I fear that my impression of you is not the same," the green-eyed head said coldly.

Mr. King took another step back, and pulled an ugly-looking dart gun out of his bag.

"This will be quite quick and painless," he said.

Sarah Emily, horrified, clung to the dragon's side. "Can't you fly away?" she whispered desperately.

The three golden heads lifted slowly in unison. Three pairs of eyes, green, blue, and silver, stared fixedly into the eyes of Mr. King.

"The space is not sufficient for flying," the blue-eyed head said.

"And we are not, primarily, a land animal," said the silver. "On foot, we waddle."

"We have other methods," the green-eyed head said.

"Don't look," Hannah suddenly whispered. "Don't look. Remember how Fafnyr can make people forget?"

The children had learned last summer about this mysterious power of dragons, the ability to wipe away memory. The dragon's eyes glowed like fiery jewels, emerald-green, sapphire-blue, and a diamond-bright sparkle of silver. Mr. King stood like a stone, his arms dangling at his sides. The dart gun slipped from his limp fingers and clattered to the floor.

"He has forgotten us and this cave," the blue-eyed head said tiredly.

"Remove that . . . peculiar weapon," the silver-eyed head said.

Mr. Chang hurried forward, picked up the dart gun, and stuffed it into one of the deep pockets of his jacket.

"I will dispose of it safely later," he said.

Mr. King stood motionless, his eyes vague and unfocused, his mouth slightly open.

"He's like a zombie," Zachary said. "Will he be OK?"

The three heads nodded. Then they moved close together. Thoughts seemed to pass rapidly from one to the other. The golden wings drew in and folded. The dragon's body settled to the floor. Then two of the heads slowly curled downward, positioning themselves on the dragon's shoulders. Green and blue eyes closed. The heads were asleep. The silver-eyed head remained awake, gazing sadly at Mr. King.

"He is quite well," the silver-eyed head said. "He will recover shortly. You must take him away. Lead him back to the beach."

"Fafnyr, this is Mr. Chang," Hannah said hastily, remembering her manners.

"I am honored, Dragon Friend," the dragon said.

Mr. Chang bowed low.

"As am I," he said.

"You were all awake at the same time," Sarah Emily said suddenly. "All three of you. I didn't know you could do that."

The golden head nodded regretfully. "In times of great danger," it said. It heaved a weary sigh. "So dispiriting," it said. "I feel quite drained."

The head sank slowly to the floor, and the silver eyes began to close.

"You will have to excuse me," the dragon said. "So exhausting . . ."

The silver eyes narrowed to glowing slits.

"But all's well that ends well," the dragon murmured. "Or so they say."

The eyes closed. The cave grew dark.

"Where's my flashlight?" Zachary said. There was a

143

sound of scrabbling and then the click of a switch. The light moved from face to face, flickered over the sleeping golden bulk of the dragon, and then steadied on the silent Mr. King.

"Let's get him out of here," Hannah said. "Before he wakes up."

Until We Meet Again

Mr. King caused no trouble. He followed the children and Mr. Chang as if he were a robot, doing as they did, edging around the rocky shelf that surrounded the crest of Drake's Hill, climbing down the stone steps, and docilely following them down the grassy slope of the hill to the sandy beach. Beyond them, on the gray water, the white yacht rode at anchor. Mr. King stood facing the water, staring blankly at nothing.

"What now?" Sarah Emily said. "Mr. Chang can't take him back acting like this."

"Look," Zachary said. "I think he's waking up."

Mr. King suddenly shook his head as if he were dazed. He rubbed a hand confusedly across his eyes. Then he looked at the children and smiled as if he had never seen them before.

"How do you do?" Mr. King said. "My name is J.P. King, and this is my compatriot Mr. Chang. We were

just passing by"—he waved a hand toward the ocean—
"touring in my yacht. This is a beautiful island. Are visitors allowed?"

The children stared at him dumbly for a moment.

Hannah swallowed. Then she said, "No, I'm so
sorry. This is a private island. It belongs to our great-
great-aunt, who does not allow any visitors."

"A pity," Mr. King said. "But I can see why she should
want to keep such a lovely place unspoiled. We must be
going, Chang."

He nodded briskly to the children, then walked
across the beach toward the little white motorboat that
had been dragged up onto the shore.

Mr. Chang lingered behind. Quietly he turned to the
children and bowed.

"You are worthy Dragon Friends," he said. "I will be
in touch."

"What will you tell the crew?" Sarah Emily asked.

Mr. Chang gave her a small enigmatic smile.

"I will tell them," he said in his gentle whispery
voice, "that Mr. King was sadly mistaken about the
island. There was nothing here of interest after all."

A letter arrived from Aunt Mehitabel, written in raspberry-
pink ink, filled with underlinings and praise:

Dear Children,

I <u>wish</u> I could have been there to help you, but you seem to have managed <u>beautifully</u> on your own, with, of course, the help of the <u>gallant</u> Chinese gentleman, whose letter arrived shortly after yours. I look forward to meeting him sometime in the near future. We may be, I believe, <u>kindred spirits.</u>

<u>Many</u> congratulations on a <u>dreadful</u> danger defeated!

With <u>deepest</u> affection and admiration,
Aunt Mehitabel

The vacation was nearly over. Mother and Father were flying from London to Boston and would arrive on the next day. Then they would drive to Chadwick to meet the children and Mr. Jones. It was almost time to leave the island.

"I don't think we managed so beautifully," Zachary said. "Fafnyr almost got captured."

"But he wasn't," Sarah Emily said.

Hannah sighed. "I know what you mean," she said. "I don't think we did very well on the reasoning parts. You know, weighing all the alternatives and stuff."

"Zachary figured out who Mr. King really was," said Sarah Emily.

"That was just lucky," Zachary said.

"We've got time for one last visit to Drake's Hill," Hannah said.

"Fafnyr's probably asleep," said Zachary.

"I don't care," Sarah Emily said. "Let's go anyway. I just want to see him. I want to see that he's all right."

"After all that's happened," said Zachary, "I wouldn't blame him if he decided to leave the cave forever."

The day, their last on the island, was gray and gloomy. The beach was shrouded in fog. They climbed the stone steps leading to the top of Drake's Hill and circled the shelf leading to the broad platform above the ocean. The water below them was gray, cold, and empty. The white yacht was gone. Switching on the flashlight, the three children quietly entered the dragon's cave. They walked slowly inward and downward, the flashlight swooping to and fro, waiting to see the first flash of gold. Then there it was, suddenly, in the darkness, the dazzle and glitter of dragon scales. But the great dragon did not awaken. There was no movement on the cave floor, no light-blooming flame.

"Maybe he just doesn't want to speak to us anymore," said Hannah.

"That would be terrible," said Sarah Emily. Her voice quavered.

"Let's leave him a note," said Zachary. "He'll find it when he wakes up. We can tell him that we tried to do our best."

"That we're sorry we ever listened to Mr. King," Hannah said. "That we should have protected him better."

"No," Sarah Emily said suddenly. "Don't say that. Just tell him that we love him always and we hope we'll see him again soon."

They wrote the note on a page torn out of Zachary's notebook. Each of the children signed his or her name.

Sarah Emily anchored the note under a rock next to the dragon's front claws.

"He'll see it first thing," she said, "right when he opens his eyes."

They stood quietly for a moment, watching the golden dragon sleep. Then they turned and softly made their way out of the cave. The flashlight in Zachary's hand made sweeping yellow blobs of light against the cave walls.

Sarah Emily trailed reluctantly behind, looking back over her shoulder.

"Goodbye, Fafnyr," she whispered.

Suddenly a narrow beam of light pierced the darkness. A single neon-green eye cracked sleepily open.

"*Au revoir,* my dear," the dragon murmured. "And thank you."

149

Sarah Emily hurried to catch up with Zachary and Hannah. Without speaking, each lost in thought, they descended Drake's Hill and set off along the little path leading back to Aunt Mehitabel's house.

Finally Sarah Emily broke the silence. "Hannah," she asked, "what does *au revoir* mean?"

"It's French," Hannah answered. "It means 'until we meet again.'"

ACKNOWLEDGMENTS

Many thanks to all who have helped in the making of this book, among them Josh and Caleb Rupp, who imaginatively consulted; Ethan Rupp, who patiently and repeatedly fixed the computer; Cynthia Platt, my editor, who—as always—gave invaluable and supportive advice and never once used a red pencil; and all the kind and creative book people at Candlewick. Special thanks also to Elizabeth Bluemle and Josie Leavitt of the Flying Pig, Dragon Friends extraordinaire; and to my husband, Randy, for everything.

Don't miss the early adventures of Hannah, Zachary, and Sarah Emily, now available in paperback!

The Dragon of Lonely Island
Hardcover ISBN 0-7636-0408-9
Paperback ISBN 0-7636-2805-0

And look for the latest novel by Rebecca Rupp!

Across the Blue Moon
In Which Time is Lost, Then Found Again

Hardcover ISBN 0-7636-2544-2

COMING SOON!